Finding Home
Paperback Copyright © 2022 Lorhainne Ekelund
Editor: Talia Leduc

All rights reserved.
ISBN-13: 978-1998775002

Give feedback on the book at:
lorhainneeckhart@hotmail.com

Twitter: @LEckhart
Facebook: AuthorLorhainneEckhart

Printed in the U.S.A

Finding Home

THE STREET FIGHTER
BOOK ONE

LORHAINNE ECKHART

What happens when a family loses everything and has no place to go?

Terrance Mack has a wife and two young boys. Never in a million years did he expect to find his family living on the streets, with no home, no jobs, in a position where everything they owned has been taken from them in the cruelest of ways. As the family struggles to stay together, they encounter a hard and unfriendly way of life, having to move from town to town, being harassed by the police and by locals, and confronting danger each day. Living on the streets is nothing as he expected.

All Terrance wants for his family is for someone to give them a chance—a chance for a new beginning, a roof over their heads, the opportunity to once again build a life without constant fear, having to look over their shoulders, feeling as if the rug will continue to be yanked out from under them again and again.

The worst is seeing the light in his wife's eyes slowly diminish, along with the hope they once had. Terrance carries a constant weight, and every day brings a new challenge as doors close and they're forced to move on. Even though they've stayed together, finding a place to stay has forced the family into survival mode, living one day at a time. The dignity Terrance once took for granted has become something he struggles to hold on to as he dreams of one day being able to have a peaceful night's sleep.

CHAPTER
One

It was the cold that got to him, the sound of his wife weeping, the desperation in his children's faces as they looked to him to fix something he didn't know how they'd fallen into.

Terrance took in the tent, the tarps around them. He stood near the fire, holding his hands up to warm them, lingering next to people he didn't know. His wife was still sleeping, he knew, but he spotted his eldest son, John, whose eleventh birthday was tomorrow. He wore a heavy black coat and trudged his way through the snow, heading right for him.

"Your mom and brother still asleep?" Terrance said.

John leaned against him, and Terrance rested his arm around him, knowing they were being watched by someone across the fire. He did his best to avoid the man with the black knit cap, dark eyes, and beard, who he was sure would kill him without a second thought.

"Greg said he was too cold," John said. "Mom is awake, though, I think. I'm hungry. She said to tell you the bottled water is frozen, and Greg ate the last of the peanut butter and bread."

Terrance took in his son's light blue eyes and the dirt on his face, hearing the words he wished he'd never have to hear.

"The shelter is passing out sandwiches at one today," said a woman standing next to them by the fire. "Get over there early, because they run out fast. There's not enough. Some take three or four so they can eat for a few days. Food's passed out three times a week." She was bundled up in an old red coat, a blanket around her, and a heavy wool hat. Her face was lined and aged, with the same lost look of everyone in the camp. "Saw you and your family come in here last night. Where're you from?"

He could feel that man on the other side of the fire watching him, listening to everything. Who he was, he didn't know, but he figured he likely controlled who stayed and who left in this camp.

"Missoula, Bozeman, then Livingston for a few nights," Terrance said. "Heard Billings had some housing I could get for my family, some work."

The woman gave what sounded like a laugh. "Not sure who you heard that from, but the shelters have wait lists. It's first come, first served, if you think it would be better than out here. For housing, the little there is has a very long wait list, too, and again, conditions are not much better than living on the street." The woman sounded so matter of fact.

Meanwhile, the man, whose name he wished he knew, didn't pull his gaze from him. It was the kind of look that had him pulling his son closer to him.

"See you have a family, a wife, two boys?" said a young man nearby, staring at him.

Terrance wondered how old he was. All bundled up, he

didn't look more than sixteen, maybe seventeen. He never asked for names anymore, just something that had come with looking over his shoulder and not being able to remember the last time he'd actually slept.

"Hey," the young man said to John, gesturing, and Terrance realized he wasn't waiting for an answer from him. "You're lucky to have two parents. Most here don't have anyone."

He could feel how tense his son was. He was thinking about what the woman had said about housing. Even the shelter he'd found just the day before had a sign posted out front, saying it was full.

"Is there a women's shelter, at least?" Terrance said. Maybe then his wife and boys could sleep someplace warm tonight, have a shower and something hot to eat.

"Again, it's likely full," the woman said. "You can try over by the Y, but it's first come, first served." She glanced over to the young man across the fire. "Is the soup kitchen running today?"

"Nope," he replied. "They were shut down by the city yesterday, some code violation. The door was locked, a sign posted. So there are just sandwiches, if we can get them."

The woman only nodded in response.

"I'm Terrance," he said to her, then dragged his gaze over to the young man. "This is my son John."

The man on the other side of the fire walked away. There was just something about him, and Terrance couldn't pull his gaze away, wondering where he was going. He was the kind of man he didn't want sneaking up behind him.

"I'm Ian," the young man said, pulling a blanket tighter around him, sitting on an old wooden crate.

"Everyone calls me Panda," the woman said. She nodded toward the retreating man. "And that was Sarge who just walked away. He kind of runs things here. Watch out for him."

Terrance wasn't sure what to make of that comment, very aware of the sheer number of people staying there. Being on the streets, you could always find out where to go. "Is he dangerous?" he said, and he could feel his son looking up at him.

Ian said nothing at first. "That's life on the streets. Although some look out for each other, Sarge takes what he wants."

Panda lifted a dirty and cracked hand from under her blanket and pointed over behind him. "Don't leave your things unless someone is watching them, or they won't be there when you get back. Over there is where I am, and Ian too, along with a few of the kids. You're welcome to move your things over there. We look out for each other."

He only nodded as he took in the snow, the cold, the makeshift shelters, and willed something to appear to get them out of this hell. "You said kids?"

Ian was staring at Panda as if she'd said something she shouldn't have. He didn't pull his gaze from her.

"Ian, how old are you?" Terrance said. "How long have you been living out here?"

This time, Ian did look up to him. "You mean here or on the streets?"

He didn't miss that Ian hadn't told him how old he was. "Well, both, I guess. You said there are other kids here. How would you end up on the streets to begin with?"

He knew his own story all too well. He'd never understood how people could end up with nothing, but here he was.

"I wasn't always out here," Ian said, "but I have been since last winter. So long now. Used to sleep in friends' garages, sneak in so their parents wouldn't know. It worked for a while, until it didn't, and I found myself here. This camp hasn't been here that long. They pop up in a few places. We get moved out of one spot and find another. You never know when the cops will come in and clear us out. I'm always looking over my shoulder for when I have to run."

He just didn't understand how a kid could be out there. "You don't have parents, someplace you could go? You're just a kid."

"My mother died when I was five, cancer," Ian said. "I was shuffled around from home to home after that, a few relatives, and then I eventually moved out here to my father, who had remarried. Thought it would be a happy reunion, but it quickly went sideways. I was soon a disappointment, not good enough. I stopped hearing all the names they called me. Food was made for her kids but never for me. If something went wrong, it was my fault. One day I came home to find she had thrown all my clothes out. That was it for me. I left, stayed with friends until I couldn't anymore. I eventually fell behind in school, and that was when I did go. I couldn't keep up. The principal pulled me into his office and pointed out that school likely wasn't a good fit for someone like me."

As Ian spoke, Terrance could feel his own shame, considering his boys had left their friends and school back in Missoula. But surviving was surviving. "What about social services, a foster home? Even that has to be better than this."

Ian only shook his head. "They'd send me back to my dad. I'm not going back to that. As for a foster place, if you talk to Tansy, she'll tell you how bad it is—and that's if you find a place where you'll actually get fed. The good ones don't take kids like us. I'm not ever going into that system."

He just didn't understand how a parent couldn't be

looking for his kid. Maybe that was why he was holding his son closer. "I'm sorry, Ian."

The teenager just looked up at him and then over to John. "It's fine. You said you're looking for housing, work. How'd you end up out here?"

He wasn't sure why he didn't respond at first. Something about listening to this sixteen-year-old had him wondering how he'd ever get his family off the streets. "John, go tell your mom we're going to pack up, get moving," he finally said, then waited until his son was walking away before he turned back. "I'm thirty-four. Been married for thirteen years. Never in a million years expected I'd be living on the streets. I had a job, working for a contractor. It paid the bills, the rent, but not much else. My wife was laid off from her job as a store clerk when the retailer downsized. Then our rent went up, and then I showed up at my job site one day to find that the contractor was out of business. I heard he closed his company, started another one under a different name. He was up and gone.

"We had no savings. I went to a lawyer to fight for the pay I was owed, but the contractor had done it all before. I was just one of many he owed wages to. I sold off what I could, and we still couldn't pay the rent, so we were evicted from our place when I couldn't come up with the money. We had a pickup, so we went to Bozeman, hoping to find something, but I parked someplace I shouldn't have and my truck was towed. My tools were in it. I couldn't pay the fine to get it out of impound. The impound fee is likely worth more than my pickup is now. I just want to get a roof over our heads. Not sure how much more we can take."

He glanced back to see his son leaning in the tent. He didn't know why he was sharing his story with these strangers. "It's John's birthday tomorrow. He'll be eleven," he said. He remembered his son's birthday from the year before, when they'd shared a pizza after he worked a twelve-hour shift.

Ian left, walking around him, but Panda was still there, tracking his every move. "You seem like nice folks," she said, "down on your luck. You should talk to Misty at the shelter, see if she may be able to point you to a trades job or something."

He only nodded, looking around at everyone in the camp and feeling their uneasiness. "So does Ian really have no one? Foster care has to be better than this."

The woman watched him. He wondered how old she was, what her story was. "You know, being homeless for a youth is far different than for an adult," she said. "For adults, it's about losing a job and not being able to afford a roof over your head, as you said. Many think homelessness among kids is about rebellion, attitude. People think homeless kids just don't want to follow the rules. But nothing could be further from the truth. Most kids on the street are here because they have no other options. They're running from a bad home situation.

"Worse, most adults around them know there's something wrong. Many are already in the system and have been bounced around from foster home to foster home, ending up locked in a system that's supposed to protect them but has failed them miserably. They have no ID, so they can't even apply for services. As hard as it is for an adult, it's worse for a kid. Then there's Sarge, men like him. If you have something they want, they'll take it. Be careful." That was all she said.

Terrance spotted his wife walking around from the back of the tent, likely where she'd gone to the bathroom. She looked so tired. He found himself really looking at this place, the down and out, and wondered how he could find a way to get a roof over their heads again. "Thank you, Panda, but I think we'll be clearing out. I'll ask for Misty at the shelter."

The woman only nodded and continued sitting on that crate, a blanket pulled around her. The odor that lingered around her, was it her or him? He didn't know. He took a step to walk away.

"Good luck," she said, turning her head.

He glanced back only once to find her looking into the fire. "Thank you. You, too," he said. Then he put one foot in front of the other, heading back to his family. Both his boys were pulling their sleeping bags out, and his wife… He didn't how much more she could take.

"John said we're leaving?" she said.

He took in his boys in the tent, rolling up the sleeping bags, stuffing their backpacks. "Yeah. There's a shelter. I may be able to get a job or something through the woman who runs it. But you and the boys need to get a bed in a shelter tonight, at least." He wondered whether she'd argue. She had before, but this time she only nodded.

"We need a bathroom to get cleaned up in. The boys are hungry."

He ran his hand over her rounded cheek, the smudges of dirt there, feeling the cold. "Let's pack up and get out of here," he said.

He didn't know what made him look, but as he turned back to the fire, he spotted the man they called Sarge dragging someone across the camp, hitting him and yelling.

"Hey, hey, knock it off!" someone called out, and a few others went running.

Terrance knew there was no way he could have his kids out there another night. This wasn't a life for anyone. He didn't know why, but he felt as if someone could be hurt or killed at any moment, or maybe they just wouldn't wake up.

As his sons pulled their bags from the tent, he realized his wife was watching everything in the camp. Long gone was the smile she used to have.

"I swear to you, Lizzie, I'll get us off the streets," he said. "Today, one way or another, I'll find us something."

He just hoped it would be a promise he could keep.

CHAPTER

Two

"We can't keep carrying all this," Lizzie said. "I'm tired. The boys are tired."

It was her smile that had sunk him the first time he saw her from across a crowded bar—the smile he couldn't remember the last time he'd seen.

"Look, the shelter's up here," Terrance said. "Today our luck is going to change. I promise."

She stared up at him, her smile gone. Instead, her expression was tinged with the edge of anger, which seemed to be all they felt now. "Don't go making any promises, Terrance. I'm tired of hearing them, and so are the boys. We're cold, we're hungry, Greg's boots are wet, and we barely have anything dry and nothing clean. I told you before I'm at the end of my rope. I can't keep doing this…"

He could see the fear in the boys as his wife slipped to a place he hadn't expected. "Hey, I know I screwed up, but one way or another, today I'll find something, even if it's just a night somewhere for you and the boys. I'll keep asking…"

He was carrying the bulk of their stuff, a big backpack with their tent, their sleeping bags, but his wife and his boys were still struggling. They rounded the corner, and he saw the line, the same shelter that had been closed the night before. The door had just opened, and people were walking in.

"Come on," he said. "They're supposed to be handing sandwiches out."

He could feel his own jeans loose on his hips, likely from all the weight he'd lost. They kept walking, looking for the end of the line. His stomach rumbled again. "Here, get in line, and remember, make sure to take more than one sandwich when we get in there."

He had to fist his hands as he shuffled from side to side, taking in the line, the people in front of them, the few with blankets around them. They all had the same dirt on their faces and in their hair, as if it had been a long time since they'd washed. He scratched his own itchy head through the knit hat he always wore. His hands were so cold even in his gloves, which didn't seem to keep them warm anymore. The line started moving.

"Haven't seen you here before."

He had thought it was a man in front of him, but instead it was a woman who turned back. She had a blanket over her shoulders and a shopping cart of things with a tarp over it. He wondered why he had never given people like her a passing thought, though he had seen homeless people forever. Now he found himself eyeing that cart and realizing how much easier it would make it to carry their things.

"Nope, we're not from here," he said. "Heard there was housing, though, and some help. They have food here? Was told someone by the name of Misty runs things."

The eyes that looked up at him didn't really hold his

gaze. He wondered so many things about her, all the while knowing she would likely be another face that went unremembered. "Not sure. They have sandwiches, some hot coffee, a place to sit for a bit."

At least that was something.

He glanced back to his wife, his boys. It was his son's birthday, yet here they were with nothing. He took in the people now behind them as they edged closer to the door, and he slid his hand over John's shoulder, seeing the weight he carried, the backpack and the world.

As they moved closer to the door and the man standing there, holding a clipboard and pen, it took him a minute to understand what he was doing. He seemed to be counting and writing. He wore a heavy coat, a knit hat, and a gold band on his finger.

"What's he doing?" he said to the woman in front of him.

She only shook her head. "Counting. Can let only so many in, and then they cut us off. Too many to feed. City has limits on numbers at the shelter."

That was something else he had never thought of. He felt the familiar ache that had been his constant companion as of late. *Keep going. Keep going.*

When the man put his hand up to the woman in front of him and said, "Okay, that's it," the ground felt a little unsteady under him.

"Look, just let my family in," Terrance said, stepping around the woman, who moved away with her cart. Just that easily, she kept walking. Giving up seemed to be all he saw out here. "My wife, my boys… They're hungry and cold."

"I'm sorry," the man said. "There are limits on how many we can let in." He had blue eyes and the start of a beard, a mix of white and dark. He gestured to the sign above the door, and Terrance could see people inside, tables and chairs and what looked like coffee and sandwiches.

"Can I get some food for my boys, my wife?" he said. "I was told you're handing out sandwiches today."

He wondered whether the man would show any emotion. In the line behind them, people were already walking away, as if this was a familiar occurrence. But nothing about this was familiar for him. Instead, it was becoming a nightmare he couldn't wake up from.

The man let out a breath, frustrated, tired. Yeah, Terrance felt the same, but he would do anything to get something for his family. He felt like just pushing past him, something he'd never have considered before.

"Get here early to get in," the man said. "I wish I could help everyone, but we have limits now, and the city is watching. If we get shut down, we can't help anyone." He moved to block the door as if he knew what Terrance was considering.

"Look, I was told someone named Misty is running things here," Terrance said. "Could I talk to her? I was told she may be looking for someone to help fix things. I've worked in construction, trades. I can fix just about anything."

He wasn't sure he was getting through, but the man said, "Wait here."

He didn't want to look back to his wife or to Greg, his youngest. But John was right beside him, looking in and feeling the warmth coming through the door, teasing them.

"Dad, I'm cold," he said. "I'm hungry."

"I know. I'll get us in there."

The man had walked inside, and now he couldn't see him anymore. There was a second of hope. Just maybe, today he could get a break.

When he saw him again, he gripped John's shoulder harder, his heart slamming in his chest. There was a woman too, with dark hair and round cheeks, not very tall. She touched someone's arm and said something to her, someone who'd been lucky enough to get in. The man was at the door now, watching this woman's back, and he gestured to Terrance.

Her dark eyes looked over to him and his family. She pulled at her brown sweater and gestured to him. "Kenny says you were asking for me?"

He took in her plump cheeks, a deep white scar in her dark skin from the edge of her eyelid to her hairline. "Are you Misty? This is my family, my wife and kids. Listen, I was told you may be looking for help, that you may be hiring someone to fix things. I have lots of experience fixing everything. I've worked construction and can fix anything that's broken…"

She lifted her hand to stop his rambling. Maybe she could hear the desperation. "I'm not sure who told you that, but I'm not hiring. We don't have money for that. You folks new here? I don't remember seeing you before."

What would he have to say to get in that door? Kenny still seemed to be keeping an eye on him.

"Been trying to find something for my family," he said. "Was told there would be some housing in Billings, so we came here. We've been sleeping outside, but it's cold. My kids are cold, my wife… They're hungry. Please…" He'd beg if he had to, though it killed him to know his son could hear everything he was saying. When she didn't nod, didn't even shrug, he could feel the door closing, and tears he'd never shed burned his eyes.

"You can really fix anything?" she finally said.

He had to remind himself to breathe in and out. He

nodded and felt the emotion swell in his chest, in his throat. He couldn't speak. She had blurred in front of him.

She reached over and touched his arm. "I have a broken water heater. If you could have a look at it and see what you can do to fix it, hot water is something we could use. I can't pay you, but your family can come in while you look at it and have something to eat."

He pulled his hand over his face and gestured to his sons, his wife, without looking their way. They walked in ahead of him, and he felt Misty's hand on his arm again.

"And after you have a look at it," she said, "why don't you and I have a talk? You need a minute?"

He knew what she was saying. He wondered how often she had watched a grown man cry. He gave his head a shake and cleared his throat. "No," he said, "and thank you."

Three

Terrance didn't have any tools with him, but he could see the water heater had been patched—and not well, looking as if it were held together by wire and gum. It was rusting at the edges, and he figured it was past its life expectancy by at least a decade.

"So what do you think?" Misty said. "Can you get it working? Right now, we have to heat the water up on the stove to wash dishes. If we don't get this fixed, we could get shut down. Word is a bylaw officer is gunning for us."

The stiffness in his back hadn't bothered him before, maybe because the hunger was always there to distract him. It was a feeling he wouldn't have wished on anyone. He couldn't see his wife or his boys, but he knew they were in the kitchen. Eating, he hoped.

He tapped the water heater, taking in how old it was. "I'll have to drain it. I think it's likely an element burned out. This is pretty old and rusty. I don't have any tools. Lost all mine..." He remembered the box in the back of his pickup, now impounded back in Missoula. The memory ached as if it had happened yesterday, how that man had looked at him and talked to him, how he'd considered breaking in to take back what was his.

"You can use what's here, over there," she said. "Some things showed up in a donation box, some tools from someone who died. I guess the kids thought it was junk, but there should be something usable, wrenches, screwdrivers. Hopefully, there's enough to get you started."

His knees cracked as he stood up. Misty was standing there in the open door. It looked like a back room, musty and old, but he could feel the warmth, something he hadn't felt in so long. He scratched his head through the old knit cap. How many things had he taken for granted? A hot shower, a warm bed, a roof, a hot coffee…

He took in the old tool kit. The tools were from another generation, at least fifty, sixty or more years old. The quality was good, heavy but dirty. Someone had done Misty a favor. He picked up a wrench and a screwdriver, seeing one that would work, and walked back over.

Misty stood with her arms crossed over a worn brown sweater. She was short, and her dark hair had some gray. He wondered how old she was. Fifty, sixty? Her hands were callused from a life of hard work. She didn't pull her gaze from him.

"You said a bylaw officer is gunning for you? What's that about?" he said, crouching down, unscrewing the plate to the electrical. He took in the mess, the wiring, checking whether anything was loose. Right, she'd said there was no money for a new one.

She only pulled her hand over her face. He'd seen that look before, lived through that frustration. "Oh, you know that saying, say one thing and do the opposite? Well, this city council has been telling the public and the media that they're doing something to get people off the streets, giving funding, help, resources, but the ones on the ground who make things happen are of a different mind. Bylaw enforcers have the ability to shut anything down and keep us closed so we can't help anyone.

"One keeps coming around, citing all these infractions every time we turn around. He's looking for a reason to lock these doors. Thought it was personal at first, then realized hate was hate. Couldn't figure out why, but every time he shows up here, based on everything that comes out of his mouth, he isn't sympathetic at all. He's convinced everyone here is just looking for a handout. He wants all the homeless, everyone on the streets, to just go away, and he's doing his part to make sure nothing goes to them.

"You'd be surprised at the number of folks who see those on the streets as addicts and drunks, lazy. They fight against everything that would give us a helping hand. I guess I'm just on the side of trying to make a difference, but it's harder and harder when you deal with that mindset where people say one thing one minute and then stab you in the back the next. I know some developer has been trying to buy everything on this block, too. Kenny said that was the word on the street. Went to the alderman and the councilors at city hall, but of course all I hear is that they'll get back to me. They ask me where I heard it and say it isn't true, but then, despite all their denials, that's exactly how it happened with Fourth Street." She gestured outside.

He already knew this was something he wouldn't want to hear. "What's Fourth Street?" He tapped the hot water heater again, knowing he was going to have to drain it. He spotted an old hose in the corner and dragged it over, then hooked it to the spout on the water heater and dragged the other end to the grate in the floor to drain into the sewer.

"It was an old building, providing low-rent housing for many of the people on the street now, some for over twenty years. Some developer and city councilors had it condemned and evicted everyone. The developer tore it down while it was still in the courts. A few of the residents hired a lawyer. The judge stayed the demolition but reversed his decision the next day, so the building was torn down as soon as the judge hit his gavel. It was a fight the city didn't want, an eyesore.

"The developer basically got it for free. He was supposed to put in housing for the residents who were there, but instead he made a deal with the council and sold all the units at a premium for those who could afford it. Made millions. They cleaned up the area, put in some coffee houses, and the police moved out any of the homeless camping there. Leaves you with that nice warm fuzzy feeling, doesn't it?

"Some days, it seems this fight is one we'll never win. You know, the councilor I spoke to was the same one who said the Fourth Street residents would get a home again. So when he says no developer is sniffing around, I don't believe it. I have a problem with a bylaw officer who's looking to shut me down, handing out all kinds of tickets. He seems to know where to look for my problems here. I know someone is gunning for me and this place, which is the last place these folks have…" She pulled in a breath.

He could feel her worry. It seemed as if everything that had happened to him, to his family, where he couldn't get one thing to go right for them, had happened to her too. "So you're saying it's just a matter of time before this building is gone and there are more high-priced condos in its place, and the city is making sure that will happen?"

She only inclined her head.

He listened to the water drain from the heater, noting the buildup of limescale. He stood up, wanting to stretch, when he spotted his wife walking his way with a steaming mug and plate. Something about the way the coffee smelled had his mouth watering.

"Thank you again," Lizzie said as she stopped beside Misty, who only nodded.

"Wish I could do more," she said. "Wish I could help more…" She lifted her hands.

Lizzie walked over to him, and he really looked at her face. Her cheekbones showed how much weight she'd lost. Her blue eyes didn't have that spark of life that had always warmed his heart. He couldn't remember when that light had dimmed.

"Here," she said. "Greg and John are in back with some hot chocolate and a sandwich. All that's left is tuna." She held both plate and mug out to him. Tuna was far from his favorite, but, being hungry, he'd have eaten just about anything.

"Thank you," he said. "Make sure you get something." He took a swallow of the coffee and nearly groaned, missing the bitterness and the warmth.

His wife turned to walk out, her hat still on, likely to cover her hair, since he couldn't remember the last time she'd been able to wash it.

"We'll be awhile here, I think," Misty said. "There's a bathroom in my office, in back, if you want to clean up. No hot water, though."

"Thank you," Lizzie said. "I appreciate just having running water and a place to use the bathroom." She glanced back to him, then walked away.

He could see that the woman who'd opened a door for them seemed to struggle with her own problems. It was humbling, being at the mercy of someone. "So you think someone on the inside here is passing along information? You said they seem to know where to look to shut you down. With enough infractions and tickets, you won't be able to open the door and help anyone."

She said nothing at first, then ran her hand over the doorway and said, "Something like that." She nodded to his sandwich, his coffee, then to the heater. "You think it's fixable?"

He could see that a build-up of sediment had likely plugged it, and he wondered how much longer it would be until it leaked everywhere. "I'll flush it out and then check the elements, but I should have it working shortly, enough to get you by. It's got to be replaced, though." He rested the plate on top of the water heater, then lifted the sandwich to take a bite, but he stopped, as Misty lingered in the doorway.

"You said you worked in construction, trades. So you know how to fix things?"

Maybe it was the way she said it, but it gave him hope. He shoved a corner of the sandwich in his mouth and took a bite, chewed, then picked up the mug and drank it down to wash away the fishy taste.

"I can fix just about anything," he said.

She nodded and then walked over to him, glancing around the back room, which was musty and old. "I can't pay you, but I have a list a mile long of needed repairs. This is an old building, and just about everything is breaking. If you can fix it, you and your family can set up some cots in the back room to stay. You can use the kitchen…"

The knot in his stomach, which had been there for so long, tightened a bit more. He could feel his chest tighten too, and his eyes burned. He cleared his throat roughly. "That would help. It would mean everything."

She nodded, her arms still crossed, and looked around. "Fine. Finish with this, and then we'll talk about what else has to be done. I expect you'll want to tell your wife."

He pulled in another breath, wondering who would cry, her or him. "Yeah. And thank you."

She stepped out of the utility room but stopped in the doorway to look back at him. "I'm not sure who's getting the better deal here. But let's give it a few days and see where this goes."

Then she walked out, and Terrance took in his hands, which were shaking. In that moment, standing alone, he was so grateful that at least for tonight, they would have a roof and some place warm.

Four

Terrance didn't know why he couldn't sleep as he lay in the dark. Greg was breathing roughly through his mouth, John was talking in his sleep, something Terrance didn't know when he'd started doing, and Lizzie was snoring softly, her back to him.

He took in the back room, dark and warm. It was a roof, a shelter, so why couldn't he stop worrying?

Maybe because he couldn't remember how long it had been since he'd slept somewhere other than a cold tent, worrying about the trouble that lurked out there when everyone was asleep. He couldn't remember the last time he'd ever felt safe.

He finally tossed back the unzipped sleeping bag, rolled off the thin mattress, and stood with bare feet on the cold tile floor. For the first time in too long, he felt clean. Even though the bathroom had just a sink with running water, his boys and his wife saw this quiet, locked place as a sanctuary.

His heart thudded as he walked out of the back room

and flicked on the light in the old kitchen. His stomach was full for the first time in too long. He stared at the shelves of pots and pans, the old stove, the old fridge, and strode over to a cupboard by the sink. He pulled it open and reached for a mug, then filled it with water from the tap, something else it had been so long since he'd access to.

He took a swallow and looked around, feeling the silence and the trust a woman he barely knew had given him. It was humbling. Maybe that was why he couldn't sleep, because of the giant ache he was feeling now at how far they'd fallen.

There was a rattle, and he wasn't sure what it was. He set down the cup on the counter and walked out of the kitchen in the sweats he slept in every night, then spotted a light outside the door. The windows were small and dirty.

The knob was turning, and the lock wouldn't keep out anyone who really wanted in. He started across the open room with its old tables, which the homeless filled when the place was open for coffee and a sandwich. Then the door clanged and opened, and there was a light in his face—and two men, he thought. The fear hit him first, shooting down his legs, icy and cold.

"Hold it right there," one called out. "What are you doing in here?"

"Whoa, whoa, who are you?" he replied, holding his hand up to block the light shining in his eyes.

One of the men wore the heavy coat of a cop, as well as a badge and a gun. He laid a hand on him, and before Terrance could say anything else, he was face down on the ground, a heavy knee on his back. The other was standing over him. His jaw had hit the concrete first, and he felt the throbbing now.

"How did you get in here? You break in? What are you doing in here? I believe you were asked a question."

He stared at the black boot by his face, fearing it would kick him. "I'm staying here. I didn't break in. I fix things…" His arms were wrenched back, and he felt the steel cut into him as he was cuffed. "Ouch! Shit, that hurts," he called out, his heart hammering.

"Terrance?" he heard Lizzie cry out. Then John, too, yelled, "Dad?"

He turned his head, his chin and cheek scraping the floor. The cop still had a knee on him. God damn! He wanted him to get off. "I'm fine!" Terrance said. "Leave my family alone. Look, that's my wife and sons. We're sleeping in here. We're supposed to be here. We have permission."

The cop who had been kneeling on him finally got up, but though he could pull in a full breath, he couldn't move. His wrists were cuffed, and he couldn't remember ever having been so uncomfortable.

As the cop walked toward his wife, her eyes were wide, and his sons' faces were pale. Of course, they were scared, standing in sweatpants and T-shirts. His wife had her arm around John, and Greg was standing right behind her, holding her arm. He thought for sure she was shaking.

"Hey! I told you, leave my family alone," he called out. He felt a foot in his ribs, the jab sharp, and he sucked in a breath. "What the hell did you kick me for?"

"Hey, you were asked a question. How did you get in here? You never mind about them. No one is allowed to be in here at night."

His side was throbbing. "I told you, I fix things in here. In exchange, my family is staying in the back room. Misty —talk to Misty. She runs this place. She'll tell you. She let us stay here," he called out, turning his head back to the other cop, who was in a dark coat. He had to strain his neck to look up at the man. He had a double chin, tall and overweight, he thought, and by the way he looked down on him, he could feel the distrust

"Hey, Vern, you know anything about this?"

He couldn't see the second man's badge. He figured they'd likely broken something on the door—the lock, the frame, something else that would have to be fixed.

"Not me," Vern said. "Who told you you can stay here? This isn't a shelter, a place to stay overnight. They have to get permits for that. You can't live here."

He didn't know what to say for a second. "I don't know anything about that. I repaired the water heater. Misty said we could stay if I fix things up here. We had no place to go." Why did it sound as if he was pleading?

"You got any proof to show us you have permission to be here? Otherwise, we're taking you out of here," the other cop demanded. He was talking to Lizzie.

"Look, I told you to call Misty," Terrance said. He felt the kick in his side again. "Ah, shit! Hey, stop kicking me!"

"You really have a mouth on you, don't you?"

He didn't know what the hell this cop's problem was, but in the way he looked down on him, he could feel a hatred he'd never felt before.

"You're scaring us!" Lizzie said. "Terrance already told you. Misty runs this place, and she's letting us stay here. In exchange, my husband is fixing things. If you'll just call her, I'm sure she'll explain everything…"

"You kicked in the door," Terrance said. "I don't understand why you would break in. Are you arresting me? Let me up, please. This isn't dignified. I didn't do anything wrong."

He tensed, expecting a kick in the gut again as the cop shuffled his footing. This had never happened to him before. He could hear the other cop on his cell phone, talking to someone, and could feel the pinch in his shoulders and the cold through the open door. Why were they there? What did they want?

"Yeah, well, we'll see about that," the cop said down to him. "You calling Kenny?" he said to the other cop, who was talking into his phone.

Terrance shut his eyes, willing this nightmare to end.

"In the meantime, what do you want to do?" the cop continued. A hand grabbed his arm and yanked. "Come on, get up."

He got his foot under him and stood up.

"Sit there." The cop scraped a wooden chair over.

Terrance sat down, but his hands were still cuffed. He reached out with his gaze to his wife, who had the same expression he'd seen for too long, haunted. This was just one more thing that was stripping away their humanity.

The other cop was shaking his head and shrugging, still talking on the phone.

Terrance felt his stomach bottom out. Whatever the other person was saying, it seemed as if the rug was about to be yanked out from under him again.

"Okay, thanks, Trent." The cop hung up. "Nope. Trent knows nothing about you being here. Come on, let's go, all of you."

"You didn't talk to Kenny! You said you were calling Kenny! Or call Misty. Who is Trent…?" Terrance yelled out, knowing he didn't make any sense.

He thought he heard Greg crying as the other cop grabbed his arm and yanked him up, almost dragging him, but there was no way he was letting him take him out of there.

"What is this?" he yelled. "You leave my family alone—"

He felt the punch in his stomach as he was slammed against the doorframe. His knees buckled. He wasn't sure who screamed, who was crying, but he'd never felt so damn tired.

For a moment, there was just spinning, a sense of surrealness, and then the cold concrete.

CHAPTER
Five

"Here, put this on your head."

The hand was dark, the voice soft. He felt a cloth being pressed to his head and realized he was sitting in a hard wooden chair, not cuffed anymore, a hand on his shoulder. He took the cloth, his hand shaking. Blood dripped from his head, down his face.

Misty looked down at him. The scar on her face seemed to make her who she was. There was a story there, he thought.

Others were there, talking in the background—a radio, noise. Where was his wife?

"Where're Lizzie and my boys?" He pulled his hand away, holding the cloth. Blood oozed down over his left eye.

"We're fine, Terrance." Lizzie appeared in his line of sight, a sweater pulled over her shirt.

He spotted the cops across the room. They were talking to a man with a beard in a dark coat. A hand was over his again, pressing the cloth to his head. Then a light flashed in his eyes, a paramedic?

"He should really go to the hospital and get checked out." The man was lanky, younger than him, with dark hair that stuck out from under a knit hat.

"What happened? Who called you? They were arresting me, I think. Who are they?" He was having trouble forming a simple question, considering he'd never felt this rattled. He'd hit his head, maybe, and the throbbing in his side was a reminder of the kick from the cop he found himself staring at from across the room, whose expression was stoic. People were talking around him again, and a hand touched his shoulder.

"Hey, the paramedic is right," Lizzie said. "You should go to the hospital, get checked out. He said you probably need stitches." She gestured to her head.

"I'm not leaving," he said. "Please tell me what's going on. Why would they break in here? I told them we were allowed to be here. That cop over there did this." He could hear the anger in his words.

"They saw the light on and said they came in to see who was here," Misty said. "I should have told you to keep it off. Never expected this, Terrance. I'm sorry. Kenny is talking to them, but they're pushing some bylaw. Because this isn't housing or a shelter, no one is supposed to be living here."

There it was, that feeling as if the rug was about to be yanked from under him again.

"So what is this, then?" Terrance said. "Do we have to go? Is that what you're saying?"

Misty firmed her lips. He could see she wasn't happy, but he sensed there was something else at play.

The paramedic pulled the cloth away and taped a bandage over his head, then pulled his gloves off. "First things first, you need to get your head looked at," he said. "Are we going to the hospital?"

Terrance could no longer see the cops by the door, his view blocked by the paramedic. What had happened? They had been dragging him out, not listening to him, looking down at him with such hate.

He touched his head and gave it a shake. "No, I'm fine. I'm not going anywhere. Those cops there wouldn't listen. They did this."

Though Misty was looking down at him, the paramedic glanced away as if uninterested in addressing his comment.

"Terrance, they said you fell," Misty said.

Lizzie glanced over at her, her expression unreadable. She wouldn't look at him.

"Lizzie, you saw what he did," Terrance said. "The cop… They wouldn't believe us. I told them to call you, Misty. Who called you?"

Why did he feel as if he needed to shut his eyes for a moment?

"You'd hit your head," Misty said. "I just got here, and they were helping you into the chair. Kenny had called me, said there was a disturbance. I live only a few blocks from here. Kenny is talking to them now. They wanted to press charges."

He wasn't sure he'd heard her right. "For what? I didn't do anything wrong."

Lizzie said something in a low voice to the boys, and they walked away. She looked so uncomfortable. What the hell was going on?

Misty appeared grim, unhappy, the same look he'd seen on her face when he first met her, standing outside, hat in hand, begging for someone to give a damn. He felt for a moment as if they were soon to be back outside, trying to figure things out. He didn't think he could do it again.

The paramedic walked away and over to the door. Lights were flashing outside.

"They said you fell, that you resisted," Misty said.

"Lizzie, you saw them…" Terrance started. So that was why his wife seemed so off.

"Terrance, you have to let it go," she said. "Misty, you said Kenny is smoothing things over with them?"

He dragged his gaze between his wife and Misty, who was nodding, looking over to Kenny. The man was gesturing to him, but the two cops were standing there, not appearing the least bit apologetic.

"You're asking me to let go of the way they cuffed me after tossing me on the ground, kicking me in the ribs, punching me in the stomach? Now they're saying I—what, hit my own head, that I resisted, that I fought back? I was cuffed, and they dragged me. Maybe I struggled. I don't remember. You're telling me this is somehow okay?"

Misty stepped around in front of him. His heart thumped, and for a moment he realized how loud he had been. But damn them! He wanted them to hear, to know that he knew what they'd done and it wasn't okay. They had made him feel so terrified for his family.

"Look, I don't say this lightly, but you won't win," Misty said. "Right now, they're citing a lot of issues that could make life more difficult for you. Bylaw officers could even come down here and shut this place down, and then where will you and your wife be?"

"How're we doing over here?" Kenny said, approaching before he could respond. The two cops were behind him.

"Terrance should go to the hospital to have his head checked out," Misty said.

"I don't have insurance, so a bandage will suffice. I'm sure my head is fine," he cut in.

Misty pulled in a breath, shooting him an edgy look.

"It will be a county hospital, so you won't have to worry about insurance," Kenny said. "You should go. Your family will be fine here."

He glanced back to the two cops. The big one with the round face looked from Lizzie to him. He didn't let his gaze linger too long, and he wasn't sure what that was about. He still felt the throbbing where the cop's boot had kicked him. "So I take it an apology isn't coming," he said.

No one said anything for a moment.

"Are we going to have a problem here?" said the asshole cop who'd ground him into the ground. When his eyes flicked over to him, he saw it again, the hate.

Kenny lifted his hand as if to hold the cop back. "No, he's fine, I assure you. Look, Pat, I'll see to it he gets to the hospital. Thanks for the call…"

Then Kenny was walking the cops to the door, where the paramedic was still standing.

Misty watched the cops and then dragged her gaze back to him. "We'll talk about this later, but you need to go to the hospital. Kenny said he'll follow you and bring you back after you're checked out. I know you're angry, Terrance, and you have every right to be, but again, it's your word against theirs. This isn't a fight we can win. There are too many people lobbying to shut me down, and then I can't help anyone."

She lifted her gaze to his wife, who only nodded and then stepped closer until it was just the two of them.

"Lizzie, you saw what those cops did…"

"Terrance, stop," she said in a low voice, shutting her eyes. He could see how frayed her nerves were. "Look, I saw what they did, but Misty is right. You have to let it go. We don't have a voice in this, and no matter what you or I say, you'll end up charged with something and in jail, where you'll be no good to us. What would me and the boys do? Just forget it—for me, please."

He'd never heard the kind of fear that was in his wife's voice now. She was trembling, so he reached out to her and rested his hand on her arm.

"It wasn't okay, Lizzie…"

"I know that, and no one here is saying otherwise. But this is about us and where we are. We have nothing, and if we're forced to leave this place and go back out there…" She stopped talking. From her tone, he knew he wasn't going to like what else she had to say.

"What, Lizzie, you think I want that?"

She firmed her lips and shook her head, not looking at him for a second. When she did, a tear glistened. "I'm saying I can't go out there. I won't go out there again and live like that. I'll end it first. I know that sounds selfish. I never understood how people could get to the point of not wanting to be here anymore, finding it easier to just end it, but I'm there. I understand now."

It took him a second to realize what she was saying.

"So for my sake, and for the boys, let it go."

He just stared at his wife, whom he loved more than anything. He saw that she meant what she said. "I'll go to the hospital," he finally replied. "You sure you're okay here?"

She let out a heavy sigh that sounded too much like relief, then offered him a hopeful smile that didn't reach her eyes. "Yeah, of course. We'll be fine."

He could have argued differently, because the one thing they weren't was fine in any way. No, they were in fact a long way from being okay.

"You have someone to drive you?" the ER doctor said, offering Terrance only a passing glance as he typed notes into an iPad.

Terrance didn't know what to make of the way the doctor's dark eyes were looking at him. Was he making sure he had a friend or that he didn't stir something up? He wasn't sure.

"Sure, there's someone here," he said.

The doctor was young, with dark hair. Terrance couldn't remember what he'd said his name was. He turned back to his iPad and continued typing with his finger. "So everything looks good," he said. "If there's any blurriness, dizziness, or nausea, then have someone bring you back, but I don't see anything to warrant a head CT. It looks like a mild concussion and a few stitches. Next time, be careful with the door."

The way the doctor tossed out that last remark had Terrance's anger festering inside him again, making him want to lash out. It just wouldn't go away. Anger was anger, and the feeling of having someone's boot on his neck was becoming too normal, something he'd never felt before his life took a downward spiral.

Fuck you! said the voice in his head. But it was a good thing his lips hadn't moved, he thought, as he took in the frown and the dark expression staring back at him. The doctor's blue scrubs were faded and worn.

It was pure instinct that had him dragging his gaze to the half-open curtain, spotting the balding head of Kenny, who was still in a dark jacket, leaning against the nurses' station, talking to two nurses. He heard laughter.

He watched as one of the cops, the one who had tormented him, walked over to Kenny and joined in as if they were all friends—the teasing, the laughter, the smiles, the kind of joking that had Terrance gripping the bed with his fists. What the hell? Was this a game to them?

The hollowness in the pit of his stomach was a reminder that he hadn't grown up with this feeling that he didn't matter. And now it wasn't just a feeling. Now he knew he didn't.

"Mister Mack, did you hear me?"

He heard the snap of the rubber gloves, and the doctor, tall and lanky, stared at him. Impatience was what he heard in his voice. He didn't know what the doctor was thinking, as everything about the visit had been efficient and quick, and the story of what had happened had come from the cop. Was this how it worked?

"Yes, I heard you," he said. "I'm fine, but I didn't fall and hit the door. I heard what he said. What that cop said was a damn lie to protect his ass. This, here, is because of him. He did this to me. But then, I can tell by the way you're looking at me that you'll believe him over me, or maybe you think I deserve this…"

"Excuse me, Doc," interrupted the other cop, who

must have been standing out there, listening. "Did you make sure to run a tox screen for alcohol or drugs?"

Terrance just stared at him. Then he couldn't help the laugh that seemed to come from nowhere, rumbling low in his chest. He hung his head and shook it.

"Everything came back clean," the doctor said.

When Terrance lifted his head again to the cop who stood there, his hands on his belt as if waiting to do something, he was nodding. Terrance made himself look back to the doctor. He wondered how well the man knew the cop.

Where were his wife and his boys? Back at a shelter they couldn't leave. She wouldn't forgive him if he didn't let this go.

"You know damn well I wasn't drinking or doing drugs," Terrance said. "Yet you're trying to create a story or imply something about me because of what you did. You tormented me, my family, all because we were staying someplace you broke into. You cuffed me and dragged me into a wall…"

"Terrance." The deep voice was sharp and cutting. Kenny stepped in and around the cop, his gaze going right to him. He didn't miss the warning in his voice, but he was too damn angry.

Terrance dragged his gaze back to the doctor, who was still standing there. "Just to be clear here, I'm not uneducated, and I'm in full control of my faculties. I'm not confused or under the influence of anything. Either way, I'm pretty sure you can't share my test results with him." He gestured sharply toward the cop.

The cop swore under his breath, but Terrance didn't look his way, because looking at that cop would convince him he couldn't let this go. The doctor dragged his gaze from Kenny to the cop, and Terrance wasn't sure what he was seeing.

"Or did I miss something here?" he continued. "You can't discuss my treatment at all without my consent, or have privacy laws suddenly changed? In fact, I'm pretty sure all of this is a violation of my rights…"

"Okay, Doc, is he good to go?" Kenny rested his hand on Terrance's shoulder.

"He's good," the doctor said, taking a step back and lifting his hands, one still holding the iPad. It was a motion he was familiar with, that of someone who wasn't getting involved. The doctor hesitated, then gestured to him quite abruptly. "You know what, Mr. Mack? Yes, you are right, but considering you were brought in by the police because of a disturbance…" The doctor dragged his gaze back over to the cop, who was still standing right there in his business.

Terrance could see he was already on the cop's bad side, and he should have cared. Maybe that was why he was gripping the thin mattress of the gurney so hard. "Really? They were the ones who broke into the shelter where my family and I have—"

"Terrance, maybe we should go see how your wife and kids are," Kenny said, cutting in quite sharply. He slapped Terrance's shoulder again, then gestured to the doctor. "Thanks, Doc. We'll take it from here."

The doctor nodded at the dismissal and strode out, brushing the curtain open wide.

Kenny's hand was still on his shoulder, as if warning him to keep his mouth shut, as he turned to the cop and said, "Thanks again, Pat, but I've got it from here. Give my best to Erica."

Terrance remained on the gurney and dragged his gaze over to the cop. So his name was Pat. He took in the double chin and the way his eyes flicked at him with the kind of warning he knew he shouldn't ignore.

The cop looked over to Kenny. "Will do. You should come down and have a beer with the boys. We can catch up."

The two shook hands in front of him, and Terrance felt the knot in his stomach squeeze again.

The cop turned away and took a step before stopping in the opening of the curtain. He turned back to Terrance. "You should listen to Kenny, here. We're not going to have a problem, are we?"

He realized it wasn't a question, but he knew he was expected to answer. "Depends, I guess, on what you consider a problem, Officer," he said with a ton of sarcasm.

The cop made a face and shook his head. "Now, listen here…"

"Hey, hey now, Pat, I got this," Kenny said. "You know he's just a little rattled. Time to call this a night."

Terrance watched as Kenny moved the cop out of the curtained-off area. Then he slipped off the gurney, seeing the dried blood on his sweatpants and his shirt. He heard the curtain being dragged closed and took in the face of the man who had brought him there. Kenny's eyes were an odd shade of blue, and for a moment they seemed so cold. Terrance reached for his dirty old coat on the chair and shrugged it on.

"You have to let it go," Kenny said.

Terrance rested a hand on the gurney. "You want me to give that cop a pass for what he did? He had me on the ground, cuffed, and didn't think twice about driving his boot into my ribs, kicking my head, dragging me out. I didn't fall. You know I didn't."

The sigh was heavy. "Okay, I get it. I get all of it, your frustration, your anger, and maybe I'm a little angry for you, but in this situation, we don't get to be angry, because all the cards are stacked against you, against us. Look, you need to let this go. Come on, your wife is waiting…"

"No. Tell me right now why you're so willing to give him a pass. You think he's not going to do this to someone else? Why are you on his side?"

Kenny was shaking his head, his hands in his pockets, and he lifted his gaze to him. "I'm not on his side. I'm on Misty's side, and the center's, because if it gets shut down because of this, and it will if you keep pushing, then she can't help anyone. There are city officials gunning for her, looking to shut her down. If you make waves, all you do is shine a spotlight. Suddenly that permit she has will be gone because of some bylaw infraction, and then she'll be issued several fines, and her doors will be closed to the public. You think those cops just showed up there because…?" He was shaking his head, and his voice was so low.

Just listening to him had Terrance parking his anger for a second. It was so wrong, and he didn't want to believe him. "And that's legal, what they're doing? Surely no one would stand for that. The media, the…"

Kenny shook his head. "You still don't get it, do you? This isn't about doing the right thing to help people. The cops who came are just the first. There will be more, and you causing a problem will put Misty on the defensive. If she's shut down, getting the doors open again will be an uphill battle, one there's no money for. Right or wrong or legal or not is irrelevant, because she doesn't have a good lawyer waiting in the wings to stand up to the bureaucrat who's had her in his crosshairs for a while. She doesn't have the money for it. If she gets closed down, everyone on the streets will have no place to go. Is that what you want?" Kenny was in his face, and his words were a splash of icy cold water.

"No, of course not."

Kenny reached over and touched his shoulder. "Good. Let's go."

Kenny pulled his hand away and Terrance just stared at the man. "This seems like a game. I'm not sure how I can be comfortable with this."

"You don't need to be comfortable with it, but you do need to let it go. You have a wife and kids. Get back on your feet. Get yourself in a position where you can fight something like this. Better yet, get yourself to a place where you won't be in this position again. Remember this feeling. Hold on to it for when you have your feet under you again, a job, a home, some stability. But where you are right now, society won't give you a voice.

"They won't say it, but it's true. You have nothing, and even though no one speaks this honest truth, when you have nothing, when you are no one, your voice won't be listened to. You have nothing to make them listen. You'll be stepped all over, not seen, taken advantage of, not heard. So if that makes you angry, good. Remember this anger, this feeling, and use it when the time is right, when your feet are under you again. Misty is giving you a helping hand, so don't burn her in the meantime."

Terrance started walking alongside Kenny, past the ER doctor who'd stitched him up, who now hesitated and really looked at him. His expression seemed questioning, but he eventually looked away to a nurse who'd said something to him, and Terrance just kept walking.

"You know that cop enjoyed hurting me. And he lied in there," he said as he strode out of the emergency room. Maybe he was pushing it. "You know him, too."

Kenny pulled his keys from his pocket and gestured to the parking lot. "Of course he lied, but no one will question him, because you're not on the same level he is. I used to work with him. I used to be a cop."

Terrance wasn't sure what he meant by that. As they kept walking, he sensed there was more, but his head was hurting, and he was cold again, and he hoped he hadn't said too much. "Will I have problems with him again? Will Misty?"

Kenny flicked the fob and unlocked the door of a pickup. "No, I'll smooth it over with him. But in the meantime, Terrance, I need you to hear me. Let this go—for your sake, for your wife and kids, and for Misty. Because if her doors are closed, you and your family will be back out on the streets, and the leg up you have right now will be gone."

Terrance let his meaning sink in as he pictured his wife's face, remembering what she'd said. She was tired, and a fight was something she couldn't face.

"Understood," was all he said as he pulled open the door and slid into the pickup, remembering the face of that cop, the hatred he had for him.

One day soon, he hoped, he wouldn't feel as if he was no one. And one day, he'd make sure that cop's boot never kicked anyone ever again.

Terrance heard voices from the kitchen and took in the smile on his wife's face as she made sandwiches. His boys were at a table, eating cereal, dressed in clothes his wife had washed in the sink and let dry on a line in the back room. He could see through the wire and coated glass that there was a line of people outside, waiting to get in.

He stared at the door and then at Kenny, who was saying something to Misty and everyone in the kitchen. There was laughter as he walked to the door and opened it. Kenny was the gatekeeper, and he could let only so many in.

The fact was that his family were just days away from being out there.

"Didn't have a chance to check in with you this morning, Terrance," said Misty. "You okay?"

He took in the woman who hadn't tossed out him and his family. "Yeah, I'm fine. Was just going to fix the outside lights and the railing out front. It's loose. I'll take a look around the building, too, just to make sure there's nothing that could be flagged and cause trouble for you. I noticed some of the wire on the window at the side has been pulled away where a gas line is coming in. I'll clear the snow away, too…"

A hand rested on his arm, and he stopped talking. "That's fine," she said. "But Kenny told me about what happened at the hospital and that cop who was here last night." She firmed her lips and lifted her head, but she didn't look at him.

Terrance didn't think he could say anything that wouldn't sound bitter, so he kept his mouth shut.

"You know," she said, "when something like that happens, it gets you right here like a giant hole in your soul." She fisted her hand over her chest. "Kenny is a good guy, but what he told you last night about letting it go, I can see it's still not sitting right."

He pulled in a breath. "Look, I know this could come back on you if I push it. I hear you. You want me to let it go, to give that cop a pass, to look the other way and just get on with things."

He glanced around the building, knowing his wife had just mopped the floors that morning. When he looked back at Misty, he wasn't sure what to make of the way her dark eyes watched him. The scar on her cheek seemed more pronounced this morning, and he noticed a few strands of gray weaving through her dark hair, pulled back as it always was.

"No one is saying to give him a pass," she said. "Lord knows I'm not, and we're angry for you. But when someone comes at you and does what happened last night, repercussions come down if you swing back before you're ready. You think this is anything new?"

The way she said it had him pausing.

"A report should be filed against that cop," he said. "I want to file a report against him, but Kenny pointed out that you're already in his crosshairs. How do you take it so well?"

Bundled-up people were walking in, and he could smell the odor of being on the streets.

She touched his arm again. "You think this is the face of someone who's taking it well?" She shook her head. "You have no idea what I've had to swallow, but you're getting a taste of what I've known my entire life. Being scared, learning early on that you're different. What's unusual is to deal with a public official who actually sees everyone as being on the same level. I knew I had to be smarter, because when you're up against something bigger than you, planning to fight it, you need to be in a position where your life won't be ripped apart if you take it on. You see this?" She gestured to her cheek.

Something in her voice had him hesitating again before he said, "Yeah. What happened?"

"A reminder to know my place." She tilted her head toward Kenny. "I was twelve when my parents moved into an all-white neighborhood. The move was done under cover of darkness. I never said anything because I could feel and see the fear in my mom. My dad always became tough and cutting when he was stressed, which happened too often.

"He bought a house, our first home, but we couldn't move in during the day because that just wasn't done back then. Moving into a neighborhood like that, it should have been a happy time, but from the moment we got there, nothing went right. The keys my father had didn't work when he put them in the door, so he had to go around back and climb in the window to open up the front.

"We finally walked in, backed in the truck, and carried in our bags. As we unloaded the truck, being as quiet as we could, the first of three headlights showed up: cops, guns drawn, yelling. I remember it like it was yesterday, the terror at hearing my dad cry out as a cop hit my mom and threw her to the ground. My dad was hit over and over. And there I was, a scared kid. This big white cop dislocated my shoulder by wrenching my arm back to cuff me.

"I lay face down on the floor, and I'll never forget the pain I was in, watching my mother kicking and screaming while one dragged her by the hair out of the house. Two had my dad on the ground, beating him, and there were more cops and lights. Our quiet move into our new house wasn't so quiet anymore.

"I heard my father yelling that we lived there, that this was our house, that he'd bought it legally and had papers. He kept yelling, 'I have papers!' But he didn't have a key because the man he'd bought the house from didn't give him the right one. Someone had seen my dad going in the back, breaking in, and no one would believe a black family could be there.

"We were in the wrong place, a respectable white neighborhood, terrorized. My father was thrown in the back of a cop car and taken to jail, and so were me, my sister and my mother. It took two days for the man my father had bought the house from to tell the cops that yes, in fact, he'd sold the house, and my father owned it. Apparently, the deed wasn't good enough, because how could a black man come up with that kind of money?

"I remember seeing my dad at the mercy of this man who had his money and had dragged his feet about coming forward. But then we were out—no apology, just out—and were told not to cause any trouble. I had suffered for two days in jail, just a kid, before my mother could have a doctor put my dislocated shoulder back in.

"Then, back at the house, the truck was still loaded with our things, and the front lawn was scattered with open boxes, broken dishes, tossed clothes. Some of our things were just gone, like my mother's antique china cabinet, two of the hats she wore to church, my father's tools, our chairs, my mother's locket, her mother's broach, and the good dishes we used. It seemed our neighbors or maybe the cops had helped themselves to many of our things and had broken more.

"But we moved in and swallowed the dirty looks, the racial slurs, and the kids who stared at me with the kind of hate that had become too familiar. We had no business moving into a white working-class neighborhood in the seventies. Bricks were thrown through our front window, and instead of 'Good morning, neighbor,' hateful words were the only things we heard.

"I watched the woman across from us walk down the street wearing my mother's hat, and when I screamed at her to give it back, her husband, who was a firefighter, came out and hit me. He punched me so hard in the face with his ring that he did this." She gestured to her face.

Terrance swallowed the bile that burned his throat as he listened. The seventies… He hadn't even been born yet.

"At school I was a minority, not welcome," Misty continued. "Even the teachers treated me as if I didn't belong. I couldn't escape the hate, the words, the slurs. Walking out of school, I wondered if I'd make it home. Then a Molotov cocktail was tossed through our window, a pipe bomb left at our house, and the N-word painted on our front door.

"My mother pleaded with my father, saying we needed to leave. I don't know if it was pride or whether he'd been fighting his whole life for what was his, but he dug in. Then our house was set on fire while we were asleep, and we barely made it out. The firetrucks never showed up until the house was burned to the ground. We lost everything.

"So I know hate. I know what it feels like to be looked down on, to hear the stories of never being able to look a white man in the eye without ending up dead. I knew they could take anything from us and we couldn't do anything to fight back. That kind of hatred doesn't go away. It goes underground, but it's still there.

"The only way to change it is to be smart. My father was a smart man, but he believed times had changed enough from when he'd grown up, seeing crosses burning, finding his brother dead, hanging in a tree at seventeen because he'd dared to look a pretty young white woman in the eye with innocent interest.

"There was my father, a high school teacher, thinking he could just move us in—but white America wasn't ready for that. They saw us as bringing crime and slashing property values. And I still see that fear in the faces of some men, women too, the fear of losing their position, their dominance, their power. That was what you got. But for you, it wasn't about the color of your skin."

The place was filling up now. Terrance found himself really looking at this woman, seeing a part of her that he didn't think she showed anyone. "Can I tell you that you give the worst pep talks? If that was meant to make me feel better, you only depressed me further. Is this your way of telling me to ignore it and move on?"

She made a face and glanced over to him. "I didn't tell you that story so you'll forget about what happened. But you need to get on your feet. You want to change things? You want to fight a man like him? Then you do it from a position where you're stronger."

That was exactly what Kenny had said to him, but hearing it from Misty, after listening to her story, seemed to give him a cool splash of water that had him seeing things a little differently.

"So where did you go?" he asked.

She didn't answer for a moment. "We moved, started over, because that's what you do," she said. "Excuse me. Kenny needs me."

He glanced over to the balding white guy, the former cop. He knew the man had Misty's back. Kenny was gesturing toward her, and she was already walking his way.

Terrance watched his boys, who were still in the kitchen with his wife. He zipped up his coat, reached for the wool hat in his pocket and pulled it on, and started to the back door.

Taking in the place Misty ran, he realized all she had done with her story was crack open a window into who she was. But instead of having answers now, he had only more questions.

CHAPTER

Eight

Terrance stood on the ladder behind the rundown building, changing out a bulb he had thought was burned out but was in fact broken. It was the second light in the back to break under exactly the same suspicious circumstances, and he'd have bet his last dollar it was done deliberately.

His breath fogged, and the cold crept through him as the afternoon winter sun set lower in the sky. The drop-in center was already closing down, and even from where he was, he could tell from the faces of those living on the streets that they would have to go back out into the cold. They passed by from every direction, mostly in the back, looking for some place to take shelter from the cold.

"You almost done up there?"

He glanced down to Kenny, a man he struggled to understand, who wore a black knit cap pulled over his balding head and a black winter jacket.

"The two bulbs back here were broken," he said as he finished screwing in the bulb and the mesh over it, seeing the corrosion. This building was so old that he could see a list of repairs that still had to be done just from where he stood up on the ladder. He brushed the snow from the edge of the roof to see that it was long past needing replaced. The shingles were missing and cracked or patched in the few places now bare of snow and ice.

Kenny looked up at him. "Not surprising. Seems to always be something. Put a bulb in and it breaks. This building is so old and falling apart that Band-Aids don't work anymore. It seems every day I notice something else damaged."

"So is this the part where you tell me this was done by someone gunning for Misty, trying to shut her down, or is this just local vandalism?"

He stared down at Kenny, who was maybe in his late fifties. His face was so pale, and the lines around his eyes were deep and heavy. Terrance was still having trouble getting his head around the idea of Misty working there with him. There was just something about Kenny that he couldn't shake, an unease he couldn't put his finger on. Kenny didn't fit the mold of someone who would have Misty's back.

He took in the cracks in the building. He would need to check for leaks inside. The ladder shifted under him, and he looked down to see Kenny staring up at him with an edge he was too familiar with.

"Yeah, I'm saying it," Kenny said. "There's always something. I told Misty that with her being on the city's radar, she needs to consider walking away. But this place is important to her. Wouldn't be surprised if the lights are broken again right before the bylaw officers show up. I keep expecting another violation ticket. She won't be able to afford to keep the lights on soon. She's already had warnings about everything—a proper railing, clearance, always something. I know someone from the city is gunning for her, and the games are only going to get worse. I reported the broken lights twice. After that, Misty insisted I stop because it was only putting a spotlight on her instead of getting her the help she needed. Whoever is doing it, it will keep happening. Anyway, a lot of snow is forecasted overnight, and the front sidewalk has to stay cleared."

Why did it seem Kenny had more to say to him, and it wasn't about the snow? Terrance tucked the screwdriver in his pocket and the broken bulb in an old plastic bag with the other one, then climbed down the wooden ladder Kenny was still holding. When he stepped off, he stood in front of the man, who he figured had fifty or sixty pounds on him. Kenny didn't appear to have ever gone hungry, not like Terrance and his family.

"I'll keep it cleared," he said as he folded up the ladder. When he realized Kenny was still standing there, he glanced back to him.

"Misty sometimes doesn't know when to quit," Kenny said. "She was offered a small fortune for this building last year, and I told her then to take it and move some place and retire, but she won't. She's stubborn. Six months ago, she was offered less—twenty percent less, to be exact—than the original offer, and two weeks ago it was thirty percent less. You see where I'm going with this?"

He stared at Kenny, wondering whether he really was watching her back. Or was there something more? He realized his trust in others had disappeared. Losing every-thing had him seeing the dirty and ugly side of people. What was it about hitting rock bottom that had him really seeing past the lies and superficiality that seemed more and more to make up reality? He had stopped listening to words, because what people did said everything.

"I'm not sure I do," he replied. "You mean it's in a

prime location, so someone has an eye on this place? If you're asking me, I think they'll tear it down and build an office building or some condos…"

Kenny stared long and hard at him, and even though they were the same height, Terrance couldn't shake the feeling that the man was looking down on him. It left him with a feeling he'd never had to experience until now.

"It's the same person, company, or developer who has a history of going into distressed areas, buying old buildings, and changing the neighborhood," Kenny said. "Yeah, it will likely be condos, with more high-end coffeehouses and a restaurant on the main floor, maybe some commercial spaces to cater to the folks who buy up the places. The front will be tidied up and the sidewalks for the block redone so it looks more fitting and not rundown, with flowers put in here and there and someone hired to tend to them.

"The police presence will pick up, and the homeless won't be allowed in the area. The camps will be moved farther out so the only faces you'll see here are those who can afford to live here. Shelters are closing, and there will be no more help for those who have hit rock bottom, because no one wants to see it or hear about it. Misty's playing with fire, and she's going to get burned. She was warned to take the first offer when it was given. If she doesn't accept soon, the next offers will be less and less until whoever it is takes this place for nothing."

Terrance was cold, and what he was hearing now had that fear he'd been carrying for so long weighing heavy, pulling across his shoulders. He wasn't ready to go back out into the streets with his wife and sons. This time, it would break them. "Why are you telling me this?"

Kenny shoved his hands in his pockets. "Because you

have her ear, and on this, she won't hear me. The fact is that there are some things she's not understanding."

Terrance leaned the ladder against the building and let out a rough laugh. "What, and you think I'm going to go and tell her to sell? Are you crazy? Did you forget this is a roof for my family? Misty is the only reason we have four walls around us right now and aren't freezing our asses off, starving, trying to find some place warm to put a tent up. If she sells, the doors close, and I'm not going back out there."

He reached for the ladder and went to walk around Kenny when he gripped his arm and stopped him. Terrance stared down at the large hand still holding him, then took in the unfriendly expression facing him. There was something about the motion that he couldn't shake, as if the man was trying to bully him. But Terrance wasn't about to back down, and maybe that was why he stared right back at Kenny, feeling emboldened in a way he never had before. "Let go," he bit out, a warning.

Kenny lifted his hands in the air, but there was an arrogance about him that Terrance didn't like. He reached into his pocket and pulled out a folded piece of paper, which he held out to him. "This is someone I know at Bridgeman Towers. They're looking for a caretaker for the building. It comes with a suite on the main floor and a starting salary of fifteen hundred a month."

He just stared at the paper Kenny was holding out to him, then took it, seeing the address on fourth street. Kenny shoved both hands in his pockets, looking past him now. But there was something in the way he stood there… Terrance couldn't shake his paranoia that this offer wasn't as it seemed. Good things didn't just land in his lap. Not like this.

Kenny jutted his chin. "Go down there in the morning and ask for Jennifer. Get your family out of here."

Terrance tucked the paper into his pocket and let the questions linger in his mind. There had to be a catch, something. "Are you offering this to me so I'll convince Misty to close this place and sell?"

Kenny let out a rough laugh and lifted his hands again. "I may be an asshole, but I'm not heartless. They're looking for someone, and right now you have a family you need to look after. I've seen what you can do and what you've done around here for Misty. You have the skills for the job, so take it and get your family out of here. You've done all you can for Misty," he said, gesturing quite sharply. Then he took a step back and shook his head. "And, if it's all the same to you, keep this between us."

There it was again, that off feeling. As he watched Kenny walk away, around the building, he reached into his pocket and pulled out the paper. Taking in the name, he felt that everything about this seemed too good to be true. Was he being played as a pawn in some game? Or was Kenny really doing this for him and his family?

Everything about this had him suspecting that something else was going on behind the scenes.

He tucked the paper back into his pocket, lifted the ladder, and started around the building to the front, where he spotted Misty speaking with Kenny. As he watched them, he was convinced more than ever that something else was going on here. But what Misty had said stuck with him: He couldn't do much now with nothing. What he could do was listen to everything and hold his cards to his chest. He never would've believed these secrets and lies before.

As far as Kenny was concerned, Terrance knew he was up to something, and whatever it was, he wasn't going to look the other way. No, he was more determined than ever to uncover what was really going on, because he realized someone was trying to stop the woman who had saved him and his family. She was looking to Kenny as a friend, as someone who should have her back, but Terrance was starting to think he might not be the savior she believed he was.

CHAPTER
Nine

Terrance couldn't remember the last time he'd seen his wife smile. She was saying goodnight to the volunteers who'd showed up to help in the kitchen. Misty had left for the day, and Terrance waited for the last of the volunteers to leave before he closed the door and flicked the deadbolt, taking in the quiet and the echoing voices from the kitchen, his boys and his wife, water running in the sink and dishes being pulled from the cupboard.

He took in the emptiness of the main room, the tables now bare and the metal chairs stacked against the wall. He switched off the light and started into the kitchen, where his wife was saying something to Greg, who was dishing up salad onto four plates.

Then she was looking right at Terrance. Her eyes still carried that lingering worry, as if another disaster could be just around the corner.

"Melinda, one of the volunteers, made a lasagna for us," she said as she opened the older oven. He listened to the sizzle as she lifted a casserole dish out, and his mouth watered from the aroma. When was the last time he'd eaten lasagna? He had to think back because it had been so long ago.

"That was really nice." He leaned in the doorway, watching John hold out two plates for Lizzie to scoop steaming lasagna onto and carry them over to the small back table, where four chairs had been set up.

Terrance stepped away from the door and walked over to Greg, whose hair was too long and needed a cut. The brown sweater he wore was stretched in a way that had him rolling up the sleeves. He rested his hand on his son's head and smiled down at him. "I've got this. Go join your brother and dig in."

He lifted the two plates with salad and felt richer than he had in a long time as he walked over to where his wife was holding a spatula, still watching him.

"You've been kind of off all day," she said. "Am I going to want to hear what you have to say?"

He wondered when his wife had become this person, who didn't want to hear about anything that could be a problem. Once upon a time, they'd talked about everything.

"Depends, really…"

"Is it about those cops again? Because I told you, Terrance, let it go. I want peace, and I'm warm and not hungry anymore, and I can finally look at getting the boys back in school…"

He set down the plates on the old empty counter beside him. "No, stop worrying. This is good news, I guess."

She glanced over her shoulder at the boys, which was where his gaze lingered. Her first instinct was to do anything to protect them.

"I told you I wouldn't make waves with the cops," he said. "I talked with Misty about it, as well, and she had a lot of valid arguments. I'm not in a position to fight them, and they know it, too. But this is about an offer I was made." He knew he had his wife's attention now.

She pulled in a breath and set the spatula down. "What kind of offer?"

He kept thinking of the name on the paper, the building he'd walked past, remembering well what the place had once been. "A high-rise condo over on Fourth Street is looking for a building maintenance person. Kenny gave the details to me this morning, told me to go over tomorrow and ask for Jennifer. He said it comes with a salary and a furnished apartment."

His wife's jaw slackened, and for a moment he thought he'd seen a hint of tears. Then she gave her head a shake.

"Are you sure it's true?"

What was he supposed to say? Everything about Kenny seemed off. Could there be strings attached? Maybe.

"I'll find out the nitty gritty in the morning," he said, "but it sounds like the leg up we need. A roof, a salary, and a new start. But you should know there's more."

Maybe it was because she knew him so well that her smile faded.

"You like Misty, don't you?" he continued.

Her eyes flickered, and she shrugged, tired, angry, and fragile from how far they'd fallen. "What kind of ridiculous question is that, Terrance? Of course I do. She took us in, and right now we have a hot meal and get to sleep in a warm spot, and with a bathroom and running water. Those little things I'll be forever grateful for. So why are you bringing Misty up in this equation?"

Sometimes he wondered if there were some things he should keep to himself.

"The day she took us in, she told me about this developer who basically highjacked some old low-cost housing building. Many of the residents had been there over twenty years. The developer had approached the city council here and managed to get the building condemned, and he evicted all the tenants. The tenants banded together to hire a lawyer because they had nothing and nowhere to go, and a judge reversed the evictions, but a day later he changed his mind and reversed his earlier decision.

"The building was torn down the second he banged his gavel. The developer basically got the building for free. He was supposed to rebuild and put in social housing, affordable, and the evicted tenants were supposed to be given a place in the new building. But instead he made a deal with someone on the council who, in partnership with the developer, sold the high-end condo units at a premium. The job in question is in that building."

His wife said nothing. He could see she didn't know what to say.

"Are you sure?" she finally said.

How was he supposed to answer? As soon as Kenny mentioned it, he'd walked over there and checked out the address on the paper, knowing it was the building Misty had spoken about.

"Yeah, I am."

There it was again, her worry. She lifted the spatula and reached past him for a plate. "You're not taking the job, are you?"

He glanced over to his sons and looked up at the ceiling, at the water damage. This place was falling apart around them. "No, I have every intention of taking it. I just want you to know, because I'm pretty sure that developer is the same one behind the problems Misty is having with this place, and the cops who came sniffing around here, too."

Lizzie scooped lasagna onto the plate and handed it to him. "So wait, I don't understand. You're taking the job even though you know this developer put people on the street, people like us, and is also giving grief to Misty?"

He wondered how to get her to understand. He wasn't sure how to take her anger. "I'm taking it because we need a roof over our heads, and the boys need to be back in school, and I need to rebuild something for us so that we never find ourselves back in the position we were in—*are* in. And because if I say no, they'll give it to someone else, and that will not help Misty."

He let his gaze linger on his wife. "She gave me some good advice, and as angry as I am, one of the things she said is that I can't fix anything for anyone now. We have nothing, we own nothing, and without that, we have no voice and no credibility. If I want to get a day in court, see to it those cops can't pull what they did again, I can do that only if I get us off the streets, get us some stability. So I'll take the job, and then, from the inside, I can figure out what Kenny is really up to. From there, I'll find a better way to help Misty."

His wife pulled in a breath, thinking. Then she nodded. "Are you going to tell her?"

He considered for a second what he was going to say to Misty, but he had this feeling he couldn't shake that this offer was mostly about Kenny wanting him out of there.

"When the time is right," he said.

Lizzie nodded. "Well, I think that sounds like the first sound plan in a long time."

CHAPTER

Ten

His jeans had split at the seam when he bent over, and he couldn't do anything about the tear in his back pocket. He couldn't remember when it had happened, but at least he was reasonably clean. The shelter was still closed as he finished shoveling the freshly fallen snow from the front of the building, knowing his wife and boys were still asleep. He remembered what Kenny had said about the front, making sure he left no reason for bylaw officers to give them a ticket.

He took in the neighboring businesses, where no one had even arrived that morning to shovel. There was something ominous about having a target painted on them, having someone gunning for Misty, when it didn't matter what anyone else did. So he'd make sure no one could find a reason to come after Misty. In fact, he'd make sure no code violations existed.

He tossed down some salt on the freshly cleared concrete and put the shovel back inside before pulling the door closed and locking it, then started walking in a pair of old boots that had shown up the other day with a box of clothes. He knew it was from Misty even though she'd said it had been dropped off.

He shoved his bare hands in his old down coat, seeing the air fog out in front of him. His face and his nose were already cold, but at least his head was warm from the wool hat he wore.

There was something refreshing about walking in the early morning, before businesses opened, seeing the snow packed here and there as he trudged down the sidewalk, which had yet to be cleared. He passed an old used bookshop, a corner greasy spoon that had just opened, and an empty storefront before he crossed the street onto Fourth.

There, it was as if he'd stepped into a new area, going from old lower-class storefronts to high-end glass. The sidewalks were cleared, and he took in someone just ahead running a snowplow. The coffeehouse with a fancy chalkboard in the window offered a mile-long list of specialty coffees he'd never heard of, the lights were on, and the employees were behind the counters. It was the kind of place where he'd be asked to leave, looking the way he did. Although the few customers inside were bundled up in warm coats, he could tell they were the kind of people who had a leg up on others, which he'd once taken for granted.

He was right next door to the Bridgeman Towers, with its sign of dark polished stone or maybe marble, which would have cost a small fortune. He took in the concrete and glass building front and saw money in every part of the place. The dark-skinned security guard who manned the door in a Bridgeman Towers uniform was walking toward Terrance the moment he took a step to the door, which he knew would be locked from the keycard access he could see.

The guard pushed it open, looking down on him, likely about to tell him he was in the wrong place. "Are you lost?"

was all the man said. He was big, and his expression gave nothing away.

"I'm here to see Jennifer. Is she in yet?" He wasn't about to cower or walk away even though he could see the confusion that pulled across the man's brow.

"Jennifer Krause? She expecting you?" he said.

Terrance took that to mean she was there, or maybe she lived there. He wasn't sure who she was, exactly, behind the Bridgeman Towers development. "I was given her name and told to come and see her this morning about the building caretaker job."

There it was, his ticket in. The man stepped back, holding the door open, and nodded for him to enter. He closed the door behind him, and Terrance heard the latch and click of the automatic lock. He took in the marble floor, which appeared freshly polished, and the dark wood security desk, behind which another man was sitting.

"What is your name?" was all the second guard said as he walked around the high-front desk and lifted the phone.

"Terrance Mack. I was given Jennifer's name by Kenny…" He stopped because he realized he couldn't remember whether he'd ever been told his last name. He knew by the way the man hesitated that maybe that wouldn't be enough, but then he was dialing, and Terrance could hear it ringing even though he held the phone to his ear.

"Hey, this is Clark, at reception. There's a man here by the name of Terrance Mack about the building caretaker position, said a Kenny sent him over…" He evidently was listening to whoever was on the other end. "Okay, then."

When he hung up, Terrance felt the knot twisting in his stomach as the man flicked his gaze up to him. Maybe he'd ask him to leave.

"Okay, you can go up. Tenth floor, penthouse."

Terrance took in Clark's nametag as he walked back around the desk and gestured to the three elevators, then walked with him under the high ceiling, past leather sofas on a green and gold area rug and artwork on the walls. Clark pushed the button for the elevator and gestured for Terrance to step in ahead of him. He held the elevator door open and slid a keycard where the buttons were, then pressed for the tenth floor.

"Suite 1006, on the right," he said. "There are only two suites on the top floor."

Then Clark stepped back and pulled his hand away to let the door close. The elevator started moving, and Terrance took in the brass and metal, how clean it was, with not even a fingerprint anywhere. He glanced at his image before the elevator slowed and opened to reveal light carpeting and a large waiting area with two leather sofas, a sofa table, a couple of potted plants, and more art, which he knew had to be worth a fortune.

He took in his image again in the mirror above a table with a huge vase and flowers against the wall, hesitating a moment because he really did look as if he didn't fit. He could see the hole in his wool hat, and his dark coat needed cleaning, and he knew his hands were pretty marked up. Then he took in the double door to 1006, fisted his hand, and knocked.

Only a second or two passed before it opened, and he took in a dark-haired woman, her skin a lighter hue of dark, holding a mug of coffee, wearing white sweats.

"You must be Terrance?" She was tall, and her voice was quite direct.

He pulled off his hat and ran his fingers through his hair, which was shoulder length and needed a cut. "Yes. Kenny gave me your name and said you were looking for a building caretaker?"

She stepped back, holding the door open. "That's right. Come in. Can I get you a coffee?"

The fresh aroma reached him as he stepped into the expansive entryway, with dark wood and glass separating it from the rest of the place. His gaze went right to the floor-to-ceiling window and balcony, which looked out to the east.

"Sure, I would love a coffee, thank you."

She closed the door and walked past him, and he stood there, looking down at his boots. She walked down two wide stone steps, and he heard the clatter of a cup on the counter. He bent down to untie one boot and then the other before toeing them off and walking in, taking in the high ceilings, the impressive fireplace, and the open-concept kitchen, which was larger than anything he'd ever seen. The dining room had what looked like seating for twelve, as did the white sectional in the living room, all open.

When he looked over to Jennifer, who was pouring coffee from a French press into a mug, she was watching him. He squeezed his hat and wondered what she was thinking of him as she slid the mug across the island. He took that as his cue, and he stepped down and strode over.

She was holding her mug now and gestured to his. "Cream, sugar?"

He wondered if that was a test by the way she asked. "No, fine as is. Thank you for this." He lifted the mug and took a swallow, and for a second he couldn't remember ever having tasted anything so good.

"So, Kenny sent you. Did he fill you in on what the jobs are?" she said, not pulling her gaze. Something in the way she looked over at him made him feel something bigger was in the works behind the scenes, and he still wondered what Kenny's connection was to this woman.

"He just said you needed a caretaker for the building, and it comes with a suite and a salary. You should know I have a family. Not sure if Kenny told you…"

"You have a wife and two boys, and you were living on the streets until four days ago. You have a construction background, with skill in trades, and you know your way around a toolbox and can handle general repairs." She had long nails and tapped one hand on the counter without looking away from him. What was it about that cold and unfeeling gaze of hers?

"Kenny told you all that, did he?" he said. Maybe it was hearing that Kenny had shared his personal history with someone he didn't know that bothered him. He took another swallow of the hot coffee, wondering when he would have something this good again.

She didn't say anything at first, just stared at him, then inhaled. "If Kenny recommended you, then that's good enough. All the condos in the building were pre-sold, and only about a third are occupied year-round. Roughly the rest are second or third homes for people who live in another state or country. As caretaker, you'll have access to those condos and the residents' personal effects. You'll have to be bonded, but the company will take care of that. You don't have a record, I know, as Kenny already ran a background check on you." She tapped her fingers on the counter again, and he had to fight the discomfort that was waging a war inside him.

So Kenny had looked into him, run a background check. He could almost hear his wife in his head, telling him to say nothing. A smile touched her lips, one he didn't like.

"You look pissed," she said. "Didn't know Kenny was checking you out? Mr. Mack, everyone who works for my company is vetted. I won't take a chance on someone coming in here who can't be trusted. You understand what I'm saying."

He did—in more ways than he was comfortable with. "Well, I have no record, except for the ticket on my truck, which was impounded, and I didn't have the money to get it out."

She lifted her hand as if she already knew. "I'll have Kenny make a call and get your truck back for you. The caretaker suite is on the main floor. It comes furnished, with a salary of fifteen hundred a month. You'll be on call twenty-four hours and will report to me if there are any problems." She flicked her gaze over him, and he wondered how disgusted she was by what he was wearing. "You'll be given a uniform and expected to keep it clean. Your family is fine. Just be sure they understand they aren't to play in the building or disrupt the owners. If you want the job, you can start in the morning."

He hadn't expected it to be this easy. He pulled in another breath, wondering why he wasn't all over this.

She must have sensed his hesitation, as she narrowed her eyes. "This is a generous offer, Mr. Mack, unless you have other, better offers you need to consider." Her words were laced with sarcasm. "Let's be clear. This is a favor to Kenny, but there are dozens more waiting in the wings with more qualifications and less baggage."

There it was: the slap.

"Of course, I'll take it. No disrespect meant," he said.

She nodded and walked around the island, then gestured to it and said, "You can leave the mug there. Stop back down at security at the front door. Clark will get you set up with a key to the suite and will introduce you to my assistant, Kent, who should be in shortly. He'll get you to sign all the employee paperwork and run through the outline of your responsibilities."

She was already at the door to the penthouse. Terrance swallowed the last of the coffee and put the mug down, then followed her to where she was standing with the door wide open. He quickly shoved his feet into his boots but didn't bother lacing them, knowing he'd been dismissed.

"Thank you," he forced himself to say, wondering why he couldn't just be happy about this.

She nodded as he stepped out the door. "One more thing," she said. "You'll be required to sign an NDA. Do you have any problem with that?"

He turned back to the woman, who seemed tough as nails and cold as ice, and made himself shake his head and say, "None at all."

Then the door closed in his face, and he took in the wealth of this floor and reminded himself of what Misty had said. He would get himself on his feet first, then come up with a plan.

CHAPTER

Eleven

"I need to sit down with Misty," Terrance said as he followed his wife into the suite that was now theirs.

Lizzie had tucked her hair under a faded brown knit hat. He took in her face, which had always been round and full, and now he could see how much weight she'd lost. Her cheekbones, which had never been so pronounced, stuck out now, and her unzipped down coat was looser than it had been the year before. He watched her reaction as she breathed in the freshness of the brand-new place, unable to shake the feeling that he'd made a deal with the devil.

"So this is really ours?" she said.

He wondered if she'd heard him. He listened to the shouts and the creak of what sounded like his boys bouncing on a bed, and he took in the heavy front door, remembering the moment he'd signed that damned document that would silence him about everything.

"Hey, boys, do you not remember what I said?" he called out. "We're guests here. I know you're excited, but keep it down. Walls tend not to be soundproof, and you're old enough to know the realities. Any complaints and we're out, so be respectful and quiet, please."

He hated to scold his sons. He took in the second bedroom of the suite, which he couldn't believe was as big as it was. The bunk bed, a single over a double, was brand new, and the dresser and wicker chair in the corner had been staged perfectly. He could feel the hole in the bottom of his sock on the new beige carpet.

His wife had pulled open a closet that held a stackable washer and dryer. The kitchen was open concept, with an island, gas stovetop, oven, double fridge, and dishwasher, all new and steel. The living room had a sofa and two side chairs facing a small gas fireplace with a mounted TV above it.

"You know, Terrance, I hope you're not worried Misty will be angry you took a job that gets us off the street and out of that shelter," Lizzie said, "because I can tell you she won't be. She'll be happy for you, for us. She provided us a temporary refuge, and that brought problems to her doorstep, if you recall. It would have been better for her not to let us sleep there."

He didn't think his wife had been really listening to him. When had he started treating her with kid gloves? She'd never been fragile or weak, but then, living on the streets could take out even the strongest who believed they could handle anything. Terrance took in the white walls as he followed his wife into the master bedroom, past a full bathroom for his boys, with a new combination shower and bathtub. His boys were now talking quietly, deciding who would get the top bunk.

His wife dragged her fingers over a light wood dresser with a mirror. There was a queen bed with a cloth head-board and a white duvet and coverlet, with more pillows than he'd know what to do with, and matching nightstands as well as a walk-in closet that led to an en suite. He followed his wife inside to see a separate glass shower, soaker bathtub, and double sinks. The towels were a mix of white and gray. It appeared as if no one had ever lived there.

"So we can move in today? And all of this stays, all the furnishings?" She lifted her gaze to him, her blue eyes holding an edge that hadn't been there before. Her lips firmed, and he could tell by the way she sighed that she was thinking there was another test around the corner for them.

"It's now ours officially. I signed all the paperwork and am on the clock tomorrow morning." He held up the keys to the suite. "The only thing, as I said, is that discretion is important. We've been asked to use the back door instead of the front entrance so as not to be seen, and the boys can't play in the building. Quiet is quiet."

His wife only nodded and shrugged out of her coat, then ran her hand over his arm. He took in the shower and the unused bar of soap by the sink. He was tempted to close the door, strip down, and climb in to scrub away what seemed like months of dirt. He couldn't remember the last time he'd had anything more than a sink to wash himself.

He followed his wife again as she opened every closet and then continued back into the kitchen, where his uniform, a dark blue heavy shirt and pants, was folded on a small round glass dining table. There was a large basket on the island filled with an assortment of cheeses, drinks, crackers, and meats, and he watched as his wife unpacked them, opened a box of shortbread cookies, and pulled one out and took a bite. She closed her eyes as she chewed.

He took in the card on the counter, which said, *Welcome. Just a little something for you and your family*. It was handwritten, and he wondered whose secretary had sent it.

Kent had been a thin young light-haired man with a Midwest accent and a desk in a large open office where it appeared two or three others also worked. At the early hour that morning, it had been just Kent in dress pants and a white dress shirt, presenting him with more papers than he'd signed in a lifetime.

"Can you take John back with you to the shelter to get all our things?" Lizzie said. "I'm going to stay here and have a bath, wash these clothes in a real washer and dryer. Greg can get showered, too…" She was still holding the box of cookies as she pulled open the fridge, stocked with more food than he could remember ever seeing: milk, juice, vegetables, cheese, fruit, and meat. His wife pulled out a package of steak and hamburgers, he thought, from the meat drawer.

His heart squeezed as he listened to her breath catch, and then she lifted those big eyes up to him. He realized that this bonus to get his family started would have a cost down the road. He wasn't a fool, but he didn't say anything to his wife because he couldn't take away the joy he saw in her face. She closed the fridge and opened the cupboards, which were stocked with cans and dry goods. He didn't know what could be missing.

"Is this food ours?" she said.

He made himself breathe as he remembered what Kent had said: *Jennifer rewards loyalty. Remember that.* "Yeah. Should be enough until I get my first paycheck. I'm just trying to do right by everyone…"

His wife pulled at her wool sweater, which was stretched and baggy, and took off her hat. Her hair fell past her shoulders, and she ran her fingers through it. It was a little tangled and needed a wash. The way she looked down at her hands on the gray and white granite of the island counter, he knew she needed a minute in this good fortune.

"You have, Terrance," she said. "This place is lovely, comfortable, and I'm truly looking forward to our first good night's sleep in a while. But you know I'm not a fool. We've been together a long time, Terrance, and I know when you're hiding something. You've had to carry the weight of our circumstances on your shoulders alone."

She was looking at him seriously. He'd forgotten how smart and instinctive she was, picking up on what went on around her.

"We fell a long way," he said. "I know we never talked about the decision I made to hire that lawyer to go after the contractor and get the money he owed me. He'd done it before, closed up business, gone bankrupt, and opened a new business under a new name, just moving his money from one business to the next like a shell game. But if I'd just walked away, you know we likely wouldn't have ended up on the streets. We'd have struggled, but not making rent is what screwed us.

"Then, when we were living in the truck and it was impounded, I lost all my tools, and it seemed as if we started spiraling…as if I started spiraling. I couldn't find a way to get us out. I had nothing saved and no idea that living paycheck to paycheck meant we were one day away from the streets. Having and owing too much… I won't make that mistake again. This is rent free, so the money I make has to be saved. I never imagined how things work, being looked down on, seeing people stepping on those who are struggling."

He wondered at times whether his wife wanted to hear his dark thoughts.

She pulled in a breath and said, "You think I can't hear it in your voice, see it in your face? You had to make a choice to look after us. I will forever be grateful to Misty for opening her door to us. I know how worried you are about this. You didn't have to come right out about Kenny and your fears that this place, this company, could be doing something you wouldn't want to be part of. But one day at a time, Terrance. We're off the streets. This may be only temporary, a refuge for the moment, but it's one step. You'll get our things and bring them over. We have food, shelter, warmth, a paycheck. You'll keep your eyes open, and we'll get better. Just watch, just listen, and there will be a day, a time, when you—when *we* can do something."

He knew what his wife was saying. He nodded. "And Misty? I can't turn my back on her."

His wife exhaled. "Taking this job isn't turning your back on her. Listen. Do you need me to tell you to take notes, be smart? You think the Goliath coming down on her would be hurt in any way by you not taking this job? They'd find someone else, and we'd be on the street, and those cops who did what they did to you would do it again. Their word mattered and yours didn't. We'd still be there. You signed something because you had to, but that doesn't mean you're turning your back. It just means you, we, are one step closer to having a voice and being heard."

He heard the boys wander out, and his wife dragged her gaze over to them.

"John, you're going back to the shelter with your dad and bringing our things here," she said. "Greg, you'll stay and have a chance to shower first." She ran her hand over his arm.

Just then, there was a knock at the door. His stomach knotted as he started over, and he pulled it open to see the doorman, Clark, in a dark blue jacket.

"Your truck arrived," he said. "Was just towed here. It's around back."

"Thanks," Terrance said.

There was something about the man's dark eyes as he looked at him and then past him. Terrance couldn't believe how quickly his truck had arrived.

Clark held out shiny new keys. "They must have rekeyed it, from the look of this. Oh, and you'll want to move it underground where staff park," he said, then turned to leave.

Terrance squeezed the keys, feeling one more step forward. "Hey, Clark," he called out, and the doorman turned back. "Thanks." He held up the keys.

The man nodded, and Terrance closed the door and took in his wife, his boys, feeling the words she'd offered him. "We'll take the truck over and load it up," he said. "Come on, John. Get your boots on." He walked back over to his wife, holding the keys, and she nodded.

"Don't overthink it, Terrance. Go get our things. You haven't sold your soul."

He took in his son, who was waiting as he stepped into his boots. "No, but this is the first time I've felt I'm suddenly in bed with the devil, and the problem is that I'm not even sure who that devil is."

His wife said nothing as he pulled open the door and took in his new home. There was something they couldn't make him sign away, and that was his memory of anything and everything he saw.

As Terrance took in his truck, two-toned green with a long back, the first thing he spotted was the steel box of tools he'd believed he would never see again. The lock that had been on there was long gone, and he opened it expecting to see it clean, picked through. Instead he saw his full set of tools, worth more than the older-model truck, which had more miles on it than it should yet still ran.

"Dad, is everything there?" John said. He wore a black hat, and his breath fogged in front of him.

Terrance took in the clean stone of the building around him. He was still having a hard time believing they had a place to live, a nice place, with food, a bed for the night, and a job. Maybe that was why the tightness in his chest came out of nowhere. He had to blink back the mist that burned his eyes, and he cleared his throat roughly.

"Yeah, it looks like it," he said. "I'll have to get another lock for this box." He gestured to John, who shot him a wide smile. "Get in. Let's see if this starts."

He closed up the lid of the box as his son pulled on the door, and as he ran his hand over the metal of his truck, it seemed as if it had been forever since he'd seen it. So Kenny really had come through—or rather, Jennifer had. Still, there was just something untrustworthy about the man.

He patted the bed of his truck once more and then pulled open his door. For a moment, as he slid in behind the wheel, put the key in, and turned, he wondered whether the truck would start. He listened to the familiar purr as it turned over, shutting his eyes for a second. The key was new, and so was the starter, and the gas tank was full. This truck was his. Someone else had simply taken it for a while.

"Wow, this is great, Dad! I'm so excited. We really have our own place? There's a TV, too. You think it'd be okay if I watch some when we get back?"

Terrance flicked on the defrost to clear the windows as he looked over to his son, seeing how much his family had given up because of him. "Yeah. I think I might join you after I have a long hot shower, some lunch, and something clean to wear. Let me clear the windows, and then we'll get our things."

Terrance could feel the cold air blowing. The truck hadn't had a chance to warm yet when he stepped back out and reached under the back seat, where he'd always kept the windshield scraper and brush. For a moment, he didn't think it was there, but he finally felt the hard plastic and pulled it out. Up front, his son reached for his seatbelt and put it on.

He closed up the back door and leaned across the front to scrape the frost when he heard a man yell out, "Hey! Told you to get the hell out of here."

He turned to see the other security guy who sat at the front entrance standing at the back door, holding it open, yelling at someone with a shopping cart. The person was bundled up and hunched, and the cart appeared stuck in the snow.

"You can't stay here," the guard said, and Terrance couldn't make out what the man pushing the cart said in reply. He started walking over, still holding the brush, and his son sat in the idling and warming truck.

"Get out of here now or I'll call the cops and have you moved out," the guard continued. "You have five seconds." He was loud, of Latin heritage, and his hair was short and brown. Terrance wanted to ask his name.

The man flicked his gaze to him the closer he got, and disgust was there in the way he hesitated and dragged his gaze over him. "You looking for trouble?" he snapped at him.

Terrance nearly missed a step in his stride. He could see this man wasn't someone he'd want to encounter alone in a back alley. "No, I work here, live here. I'm the new caretaker." He kept his voice even, calm, though he wanted to snap at the asshole who was still staring at him as if he were no one. It was the kind of anger he'd become too used to.

"That piece of shit over there yours?" the man said, gesturing sharply to the truck.

Terrance had to remind himself how happy his wife was there, and his kids, as he stopped and made himself look over his shoulder to his idling truck, seeing the exhaust and the rust. It was the best thing he'd seen in a long time.

When he looked back, he took in the man with the cart staring back at him, and he realized it wasn't a man but a woman, Panda, from the camp. He made himself look away and back to the angry security guard, whom he wasn't about to cower under. He forced himself to hold out his hand and said, "I don't think we got a chance to meet. I'm Terrance. You work with Clark at the front?"

The man hadn't moved to shake his hand. The dark brown eyes staring back at him were filled with the same unforgiving disgust that had stared his way for too long, and Terrance felt like an idiot when he wouldn't give even a little.

"I know who you are," the man said. "That piece of shit had better not be here again. Take it to the staff parking underground in back, and make sure it stays out of sight."

Five, six, seven… he counted in his head, pulling his hand back and fisting it. The man, who wouldn't even give his name, kept his hands fisted at his sides, too, and Terrance wanted to say something to the prick, but the sound of his truck running reminded him that his son was sitting there, waiting for him, and he knew walking away was his only choice.

"And you, I told you to get this out of here," the man continued, stepping away from the door and over to Panda. His hand went right to the cart and knocked it over.

"Hey, what are you doing?" she yelled. "No, don't step on that! Stop! That's mine…"

Terrance stared in horror as the man kicked the cart in his fury, and it spilled out with a clatter. He reached for a blanket and tossed it, then stomped on an old clock until it shattered, then kicked it away.

"Don't do that! Stop!" Terrance called out as he stepped over to the guy.

Panda reached down to grab what she could just as the man kicked a box out of her reach. It was like a fucking game to him. That was all Terrance could think. What was wrong with the man?

"Hey, listen," he said. "She's going. Don't be an asshole and a bully." He reached for Panda's arm, having a hard time understanding where human decency had gone. There was nothing like that in the man, he realized.

"You're damn right she's going. What, you want some of this?" He was looking right at Terrance, still kicking Panda's belongings, her clothes, a sweater, tossing everything he could grab, ripping pages out of her books. She was yelling, and Terrance found himself looking back to his truck, where he knew his son was watching and could see everything. He needed to shut this down.

"Look, I don't want any trouble," he said. "You want her to leave? I'll take care of it. You don't have to do this." He didn't know how he managed to sound so reasonable as he held her arm and somehow managed to get her to step back.

"Or what?" the man said. "Come on. You want to hit me, don't you? I can see it in your face. Take your best shot. You a man, or what? Or maybe I'll kick your ass, teach you a lesson in front of your boy." He kicked the shopping cart again and again, another box tumbling out with the sounds of things breaking.

What the hell was wrong with the guy? Terrance held a hand up as if to calm him, holding Panda so she stayed back. There was something about the way the man was looking at them—the hate, the anger. Why?

"Garcia!"

Terrance hadn't heard the door open. The shout was low and deep, and he glanced back to see Clark.

"You need to reset the cameras in the garage," Clark said.

Hadn't he seen what the guard had done? For a second, no one said anything, and Terrance took in the mess, the destruction of Panda's things. He realized Garcia was still looking his way, and he wanted to say something. Then the man smiled and shrugged.

"Sure," he said so calmly, then took one step and another to the door. He stopped too close to Terrance and nodded to the cart. "Clean this mess up and get it out of here. We don't allow this riffraff back here," he said, a warning. Then he flicked his hard gaze down at Panda. "You come back here again, and next time I won't be as nice," he leaned in and whispered. Then he spat on the ground at her feet.

Terrance stared in horror as Garcia walked into the building, past Clark. He waited for him to do something, say something.

"You get this out of here," Clark said, looking right at Panda and then over to him.

Terrance let go of her arm and walked over to him. "Did you not see what Garcia did? He kicked her things around. What is wrong with that guy?"

Maybe it was the expression on Clark's face that shocked him. He had expected empathy or something. "We don't allow any loitering or panhandling or any homeless back here. When you're done, you'll need to check in with Kent. He's going to need you to start tonight instead of tomorrow morning." Then he jutted his chin, his gaze lingering a second, taking in the mess on the cleared pavement. "You see to it she moves on and gets all of this out of here. If we get one complaint from any of the residents, it'll land at your feet."

He wanted to swear under his breath, but he bit his tongue and only shook his head, turning back to a woman who didn't deserve this. He heard the click of the door and glanced back to see Clark was gone, so he leaned down and righted the shopping cart along with the few things still inside it.

"I'm so sorry about this," he finally said, seeing Panda's

dirty hands and smelling the odor that came from her. Once, he'd have made a face at it.

"You got your family off the street," she said. So she recognized him.

He leaned down, picked up a cloth bag of what looked like stuffed animals, and put it back in the cart as she did the same with a box of what looked like broken plastic. "I did. I guess I have you to thank. My son is over there, waiting in the truck. Can I give you a ride someplace?"

She settled the box in the shopping cart as he picked up a blanket, an old tarp, and a sweater, rolled them up, and tucked them in the cart. He wasn't sure what to make of her face as she looked up at the building.

"You know, I used to live here—well, before it was turned into this. It used to be a home for me and many others, nothing fancy, cheap. Then we were tossed out, and the old building was torn down. They were supposed to put affordable housing back here, but I knew by the fancy high-end developer that it would never happen. Affordable housing isn't pretty, and by the stone and how nice everything was, I knew it would be another fancy place for people who could afford it." She let her gaze linger on the building. He wanted to say he was sorry even though he hadn't done it.

"I wish I could do something for you," he said instead.

She only shrugged and walked over to the shopping cart he'd righted, placing her hands on the handle. "Just glad you got off the street," she said. She started pushing the cart down the alley, and he knew there was nothing he could do there. She'd get no justice, and the thought of the police flickered through his mind for only a second before he dismissed it.

"Panda," he called out. She stopped and turned her

head but didn't let go of her cart, and she didn't say anything. "You need anything, you let me know."

She didn't nod, only looked up at the building again and back to him. "You take care of that family of yours," she said. Then she kept walking, pushing that cart back down the alley the other way.

He turned back to his still idling truck and started walking, one foot and then another, all the way back to it. The windshield had defrosted, so he opened the door to climb in, tossing the brush he'd been holding over the seat. Then he took in his son, who, he could tell from his face, had seen everything.

"Dad, are we going to have to move?"

He forced a smile to his face, hearing the fear in his son's voice. "No, we're fine. We're going to pick up our things, and when we get back, your mom should have lunch ready, and then you can go take a hot shower." He reached over, feeling the warmth now in the cab, and rustled his son's head.

"Dad, that man…"

He knew what his son was going to say about the security guard, the way he'd tossed Panda's cart, his anger.

"Don't worry, he won't hurt you. I handled it. Everyone is calm, see? Cooler heads prevail," he said. Then he pulled his seatbelt on, put the truck in gear, and glanced once up the alley to see she was long gone.

He pulled out, adding one more item to his list of things to make right, a list he realized he couldn't share with anyone.

Thirteen

Terrance stood at the back of his pickup, tossing in their clothes, their sleeping bags, and basically everything they owned, whatever they'd been able to carry on their backs. For a moment, after he tossed in the tent, he glanced back to Misty's rundown old building, which had been a refuge to them, and he thought of the place they had lost, their three-bedroom house with its front porch and wooden swing, where he'd sat so many nights with his wife. In that second, the ache came out of nowhere. He thought of the kids' toys, their furniture, and how it seemed as if his family and life had been reduced to the few items in the back of his pickup.

"There you are. John said you were back here," Misty called out. He hadn't heard her walk up to him. He took in the cream wool hat over her dark hair, her unzipped down coat, and her untied boots. "He said you have a new place, a really nice place you've moved into?"

Why did he feel so guilty all of a sudden? He didn't know what to make of the way she was looking at him. "Yeah, I wanted to talk to you about that. I was offered a job, but I also want you to know I'll still help out here. I'll work around my job."

She lifted her hands and shook her head. "No, Terrance, stop. I'm just glad you found something. That's the ultimate good news. You don't owe me anything…"

How could she be so damn kind? Of course he owed her. He owed her everything.

He found himself looking away, then back to a woman who was so complicated. He wondered whether she had any idea who was gunning for her.

"You're wrong, Misty. I owe you everything. I never realized how far we fell, and there were too many nights and days where I found myself losing hope. I had to look back to my sons and wife and realize they were still there, looking to me to do something. I wonder if people have any idea that no one out there is safe. What happened to me could happen to anyone. It was just a series of things going wrong. When someone threatens your family's security, that one paycheck is the difference between having a roof over your head and being on the streets. I'm not a drunk or an addict, but I've lost count of the number of times I've been treated as if I'm worthless and have no rights. The anger is still here." He fisted his hand and tapped his chest.

She only stared at him. He wasn't sure she agreed. She didn't look away, didn't say anything at all. She was strong, unbending. He took in the scar on her face and wondered how much she hid from everyone.

"Anger is good as long as you don't let it lead you," she said. "Remember everything, but tuck it someplace until you're in a position to use it for good. I know you're angry. You've been hurt and betrayed, had the shit kicked out of you, but you get back on your feet, and when the time is right, and you'll know when that is, you'll do something with it."

"You haven't asked me where I'm living, where I'm working…"

She pulled her arms over her chest. "On Fourth, the new construction that replaced the homes of many low-income earners, leaving them out on the street. They tore the building down and put in condos to be sold to the wealthy. I know, Terrance. I can see it in your face. You think who you're working for means you're betraying me in some way, but you're not. You need to have a new start. You need to get your kids and your wife out of here. I'm going to be okay."

He let out a sigh, glancing to the back of the old building, the mesh over the window he still needed to fix. He couldn't help worrying over how much she knew about how he'd gotten the job.

"You have people close to you," he said. "Do you ever worry they could stab you in the back? I know the fight you have here, and you have some powerful people behind the scenes gunning for you, to take this from you…"

She touched his arm and then pulled her hand away. "Don't treat me like a fool, Terrance. I know exactly what I'm up against, who's on my side and who isn't. I've known hate, grown up with it, and faced it every day. I gave up long ago trying to figure out why people do what they do. They hate because of fear, and they fear what they don't understand. I know the problems that come from power. Sometimes you have to take a step back when someone is too big and powerful. When a complaint is filed against me and bylaw shows up again with another ticket, my yelling and screaming would end up only with something else coming at me. Sometimes you have to step back to see the bigger picture.

"It took me a lot of years to learn that, to bide my time. I've learned to get up and bandage my cuts when I get kicked to the curb. Maybe I'll step away and cry for a moment, but then I'll dry my tears and keep going. I won't be deterred or scared off. I will remain calm in the face of adversity. Because they're looking for me to lose it, to become irrational, to be provoked in a single moment to say or do something that can be used against me. And that one moment would black out an entire lifetime of good things that no one would see. It's hard, and I know, but I won't have my entire life reduced to that. I have people who have stepped up to watch my back, to help me…"

"Kenny is the one who got me the job, and he knows—"

The look she shot him had him shutting up. "You think Kenny is betraying me, don't you?"

His heart thudded once, twice, and he nodded. "I do."

She looked away and made a face. He wondered if she was smiling. She didn't seem upset. "You're a good man, Terrance. Look after your family, and don't let Jennifer bully you, because she will, or she'll have her people do it for her." She went to take a step. As John came around the corner, she ran her hand over his head and said, "You take care, John."

"Bye, Misty," his son said.

Terrance gestured to him. "Get in the truck," he said gently, then took in Misty walking away. "Misty!" he called out, taking a step toward her. She turned around and faced him, and he realized she knew more about what was going on than he did. "You know Jennifer?"

She lifted her chin to him. "I do," she said. "She's my sister."

Fourteen

Hot water was something Terrance hadn't enjoyed in what seemed like forever. After the longest shower he'd ever taken, he stopped for a second to promise himself that he'd never take these simple things for granted again—a shower, a bathroom, a clean towel, and the smell of the lunch his wife was making. He strode barefoot over the unfamiliar new carpet, down the hall, past the running dryer, as he buttoned up his dark blue uniform shirt. He heard the TV and spotted his wife at the stove heating soup, with sandwiches already on a plate.

"Wow, you really clean up well," she said. "Can't remember the last time you shaved."

Instinct had him lifting his hand and pulling it over his smooth face. It seemed as if everything they needed had been supplied for them. "Looking forward to sleeping in a real bed tonight, too," he said. "Smells good. I'm starving."

He pulled back the high stool at the island as his wife set a ham and cheese sandwich in front of him. His boys sat on the sofa in front of the TV, sound asleep, John's hair still damp. When he took a bite and chewed, he wondered if he'd groaned from how good it tasted.

"You eat already?" he asked his wife as she set a steaming bowl of vegetable soup in front of him.

"Greg and I ate before you got back. I'm thinking I might take a nap, as well, while you're working. Do you think you'll have to work late?"

He didn't know what he had to do. Check in with Kent to get his keys, get the lay of the land, maybe get familiar with the building. He shook his head as he swallowed a spoonful of soup.

"I don't know. I'll check in with Kent, find out what needs to be done. Did John tell you what happened?"

In Lizzie's unsmiling expression, he wasn't sure whether he saw fear or something else. "He told me about an altercation in the alley, a homeless person… She shouldn't have been there. He said one of the men who works here was pretty rough with her."

From her hesitation, he realized she was no longer that woman who would jump in and defend someone who was being taken advantage of.

"It was Panda—you know, the old woman from the camp, the one who gave us Misty's name and sent us to the shelter? If it hadn't been for her…"

"You don't need to explain. I know who she is." Lizzie cut him off quite sharply, and her lack of empathy, so unlike her, was not lost on him.

He gripped his spoon and took another mouthful of soup, then rested the spoon in the bowl. "And you think Garcia was in the right for treating her so badly, like maybe she had it coming?" He didn't know how he kept his voice so calm, not pulling his gaze from Lizzie.

She pulled her sweater tighter around her thin frame. She really had lost a lot of weight. When she lifted her hands, he knew he'd hit a nerve. She appeared to be waging an internal war, and she rested her hand on the counter and said nothing, looking down and not at him as he finished his sandwich.

"She's a person, Lizzie, just like you and me," he said, but she still wouldn't look at him. He took another sip of his soup and heard the dryer ding.

"Your socks should be dry," she said, and that was it.

He watched her walk out of the kitchen to the hallway and pull open the closet door to reveal the stackable washer and dryer. As he finished his soup, he wondered when his wife had decided to turn into someone he didn't know.

She was right beside him now, holding out his worn black socks. "I'm not unfeeling, Terrance. We've been together a long time, and I know that look you have. You think I'm horrible because I'm not jumping in to help that woman. But let me tell you something: I'm not a monster. The only ones I can help are our sons, me, us. We have a roof over our heads, and food, and I will do everything I can to make sure we don't end up out there again. You work here. You can't afford to take a stand on anything. Keep your head down. Go do your job. I'm telling you right now, Terrance, I am not going back out there, living with nothing. So you look after your family and stop worrying about the Pandas on the street. You can't do anything to help them. You have to look after your family first."

He took the socks from her, his anger simmering. She had meant every word she said, and he realized she was fighting to keep this for them. As she walked into the living room, he pulled on his socks and slipped off the stool, then headed to the door and pulled on his boots. Lizzie was back in the kitchen now, reaching for his bowl and plate and putting them in the sink, but she didn't look his way.

They should have been happy, but the tension was thick.

"Lizzie, I understand you're scared, but don't let fear take your humanity," he said. He reached for the door and pulled it open, and she was washing the dishes, busy doing anything but looking at him. So he made himself step out into the hall and pulled the door closed.

He started down the hall to where the elevators were, taking in the quiet and pristine entry, the expensive marble floor, and a man who was staring at him with the kind of hatred he'd been on the other side of for too long.

"You'd better get your ass upstairs to Kent if you want to keep your job," Garcia drawled.

Terrance knew he was already on his bad side, and he realized he'd never want to be alone with him. He said nothing as he pressed the elevator button.

"Use the stairs," Garcia called out.

He had to remind himself his wife didn't want to move. This was just a man on a power trip who was trying to break him. As the elevator dinged, he made himself start walking to the stairs, but he turned back when he heard voices and saw Jennifer and Kenny stepping out of the elevator, deep in discussion. They were walking right to the front door when they looked his way.

"Oh, you're the new caretaker. What was your name again?" Jennifer said. She wore a white wool coat, her dark hair styled, her makeup perfect.

"That's Terrance, remember?" Kenny said to her, and Terrance wasn't sure what to make of his tone. He couldn't help wondering why he was there with her. He was trying to see a resemblance to Misty after the bombshell she had dropped on him. He knew there was so much more going on, as if he were the only one who didn't know the secret.

"Oh, right, that favor I owed you," Jennifer said to Kenny. "Well, I guess that makes it so I don't owe you now —or is it that you now owe me?"

For a moment, it sounded like flirting at his expense.

Kenny laughed, his hand on the door, and said, "Give me a second to talk to Terrance."

She patted his chest in a way that said they were more than friends. Then Kenny was walking his way, glancing only once to Garcia, who was sitting behind the security desk now, quiet, minding his own business.

"You settle in okay?" was all Kenny said as he approached and stopped in front of him.

"We are. Thanks again. I didn't realize…" He didn't know how to say anything about Misty and Jennifer or ask the one question he really wanted answered: What the hell was going on? Kenny was waiting for him to finish, so he said, "Misty told me she's her sister."

Kenny glanced to Garcia and then made a motion to usher Terrance off to the side by the stairs, out of earshot. "It's complicated."

"Isn't it always?"

Kenny said nothing, not pulling his gaze. As they stared at each other, Terrance realized Kenny didn't trust him.

"I plan on going back over to help Misty when I have time," he said.

Kenny tapped his shoulder. "She'll appreciate it. Look after your wife, your kids. And a word of advice from someone who knows?"

He wondered, if he said no, would that be the end of it? He didn't say anything.

Kenny reached over and touched his shoulder again. "When you're in a fight to keep your head above water, it's always best to think first instead of acting and saying something that will have you wishing you could take back those thirty seconds. Get your facts and your story straight, and think of what's best for your family. I see you might say something, thinking you're doing right by Misty, but it's not smart. You're angry. You have a chip on your shoulder, but you need to be smart, Terrance. You have a good job and a roof over your head. You've been given a second chance. Don't blow it over your sense of right and wrong by sticking your nose in and questioning things that aren't your business. Misty and Jennifer are a no-go territory for you. Understand?"

He didn't miss the warning. "Loud and clear," he made himself say, realizing that Kenny was watching him closely. He needed to dial back his questions, his outrage.

"Say hi to your wife and kids," Kenny said. "And think long and hard before sticking your neck out, because it isn't just yours that'll be on the chopping block; it'll be your family's, too. Be happy with this gift you've been given." Then he patted his shoulder again and walked away, saying something to Garcia, who seemed to be familiar with him.

As he watched Kenny walk over to Jennifer and then out the door, he realized Garcia was watching him.

"Get going now," the man said.

Terrance took in the sign to the stairwell and pushed open the door, taking in the concrete steps. He looked up and started to the third floor. One step, two steps… Kenny was right about one thing: He needed to get the facts and his story straight. But he couldn't shake the feeling that whatever the hell was going on, Kenny was up to something. And whatever it was, he was damned sure he would figure it out.

Fifteen

The Jennifer and Misty no-go territory was exactly where Terrance was going as he trudged through the fresh snow of the early morning, which no one had yet shoveled from the sidewalks in front of the shops. His breath fogged in front of him, and he thought of the warm bed he'd climbed from, leaving his wife sleeping soundly. The boys too had been fast asleep, peaceful and warm, enjoying the first good night's sleep they'd had in a long time.

Terrance had made coffee, eaten a bowl of cereal, and reminded himself he needed to report back every morning at eight a.m. Apparently, that was when he would receive his orders for the day from Kent, as would security, housekeeping, administration, and everyone else employed by the Bridgeman Group.

He knew he had time to give at least two hours to Misty. He'd decided the night before that it would be the least he could do, and he wasn't about to share it with anyone. He pulled at his old hat, the hole at the side bigger than it had been the day before, and shoved his cold hands into his pockets as he came to the end of the street, seeing the shelter and feeling for the key he still had.

The streetlights cut through the darkness and cast an eerie shadow on the falling snow as Terrance approached the corner, crossing from an upscale new block, neat and tidy, over to the rundown and tired old street where the shelter was. He could see it ahead, the snow piled up on the sidewalk around it, the old rails that led down the walkway to the door, and the wood rotting around the caged windows he had repaired.

He felt a heaviness as he spotted a shopping cart with a tarp and what he thought was someone sitting under it at the side of the building. Then he found himself stopping at the sight of something taped to the front door—a paper? He looked up the street and then the other way, then made his way to the front door.

He took in black ink with something marked in red right across it, an order of closure from the council. His heart sank, sitting heavy like lead in his stomach. A new padlock had been screwed on over the door, likely by whoever had taped up that paper. He stared at the closure notice, seeing a signature at the bottom, and he couldn't help himself as he read out the handwritten complaints: *Noise, increased crime in the area, health code violations, and a lack of compliance with current electrical and safety codes, with bylaw infractions 416, 512, and 1620.*

"What garbage is this?" he muttered, reaching for the padlock and lifting it, knowing this time it had gone too far.

"What are you doing here?"

Terrance turned to see a bundled-up Misty trudging through the snow toward him.

He stepped back from the door, the padlock clanging

as he let it drop. "I wanted to stop by and do a few things —shovel, at least. But I didn't expect this."

She walked around him to the door and glanced at the paper taped there. Her expression said everything: She was pissed off, blindsided. Not exactly the welcome she deserved. "Well, well… The dogs are at the door, and they think they've won this one." She pulled on the padlock, and the new hinges screwed on to keep her out rattled. She shook her head.

"So you didn't know about this?" Terrance said.

"Oh, they've been gunning for me a long time. Knew they'd do something. I've been able to stay ahead of them, but it seems they're not above making things up. Crime is up? My ass. There's been no more crime down here than ever, but I guarantee you you'll suddenly find two cops citing an incident that happened here, just enough of an allegation, and one they don't have to prove."

She pulled the paper from the door. "And who the hell knows what these bylaws even are? Complaints? Yeah, complaints from everyone who wants to pick this building up for nothing. Guarantee you they'll be a bunch of made-up names."

He didn't know what to say to make this better. "I can bust this off if you want," he said, gesturing to the padlock. "Not sure what else to do. Can you call the city, this bylaw officer or whoever this is, and…?"

From the way she looked at him, he realized everything he was saying was wishful thinking. Even he knew better. "The only thing that will accomplish is to have no one call me back, and I'll waste an entire day sitting down there, doing nothing, when people are on the streets, freezing and starving. This isn't my first rodeo, Terrance." She gestured to the door. "But they've gone too far this time. Please, if you can open it, I'll pack up my car with the sandwiches in the fridge, at least. The ladies were here late last night making them. I guess I'll drive around, see who I can see, get word out. If I have to, I'll give them out from the back of my car. This is just damn cruel."

He stared at her for another second. There was just something about her strength that he envied. Damn, anyone else would have walked away and given up. He wondered if there was a point where she'd just close up and stop helping. Everyone had to have a breaking point. "Yeah, I'll get it open. Let me guess: If they impounded your car, you'd just give them out on foot, wouldn't you?"

She didn't say anything in response, and he took that minute to look around and kick the snow away, looking for anything he could use to pry the padlock off with.

"I hope it doesn't get to that," she said, "but I guess you're right. No one is going to tell me what I can't do. Seems we're in a fight now."

Terrance spotted a narrow metal bar loose at the window, and he reached for it and pulled, snapping it from the rotting wood. He walked back over to the door and slipped it under the hinge, and he lifted, putting everything into it, and popped the screws from the hinges. Whoever did it had done a shitty job, using screws that were barely embedded. He pulled the padlock away, and Misty shoved a key in the door and opened it. She flicked on the light, but nothing happened. It was dark inside.

"I see they cut the power, too," she said.

He followed her inside the darkened building, the door open behind them. "I don't think they can legally do that."

"Terrance, they can do anything they set their minds to," she called from the kitchen. "They have the means. Someone made a call to the person in charge. Cut the power, shut her down, set her up, burn her out…"

The way she kept saying "they" bothered him.

"You know who is doing this?"

There was a clatter in the kitchen, the sound of the fridge, and then she reappeared, carrying two tin roasting pans stacking one on top of the other, filled with sandwiches, he thought.

"Of course I know," she said. "I've had this target on me from the beginning."

"Here, let me take those." Terrance reached for the trays.

"Thank you. My car is out front." He let her walk out ahead of him and up the walkway to the curb and an older light blue compact. From the rust, he wondered how well it ran. As she opened the hatchback, it squealed. "Just in here is fine. You know, Terrance, I really appreciate you showing up, but you should know something. If you're going to keep coming here, you could end up with a target on you, as well."

He stepped back without looking away, wondering why she was trying to warn him. He only shook his head. "No. Sorry, Misty, but I won't be intimidated or scared off, and I don't turn my back on people I care about. Some may say it's a fault, but I need to do the right thing. Are we talking about your sister? She's the one who owns that condo, the corporation. Saw Kenny with her last night, and even he warned me not to tread into your business."

Something hinting at amusement pulled at her lips. "When you grow up with segregation, being treated as a second-class citizen, having to fight for everything that comes so easily to others, you can turn out one of two ways. You either want to help fix the world and right the wrongs, making it a better place, or you become mean and angry. You want to take from the world, and you don't much care who you walk over or hurt or destroy along the way. Apparently, I'm doomed, because I feel for those who are one step from the grave, giving up, without any idea how to get back into society. Then there is my sister. She sold her soul to the devil a long time ago. But you know what, Terrance? She can do anything she wants. She can make a call and get me shut down, ticketed, harassed by the police and bylaw officers. She can even get my power shut off. But I won't be bullied by her. I will get up and brush myself off every time, and I will get back out there. Do you know why I do it?"

He wanted to say it was because of stubbornness, determination, and a strength he couldn't remember seeing in anyone before, but he said none of that. Instead, he made himself shake his head. "I don't know. You'd better tell me."

"Because she can't win."

He knew he was frowning. "She has money, power, and resources, and you're saying she can't win?" Even he could hear the disbelief in his voice, but the way she stared at him, he could see she really believed it.

"Have some faith, Terrance. Even when I was staring into the face of evil that exists in some people, I learned to get past my fear, because fear is a poison that will have you turning on your neighbor. Good always wins, always. It may be a bumpy ride to get there, but good always wins over evil." She reached over and touched his arm. "You should go back to your new place. Be careful of my sister."

He just stared at this woman, who seemed to be fighting an impossible situation. She walked around him to the open door of the shelter. "Do you want me to close it up for you?" he called out, but she just lifted her hand to him.

"No, I got it. You go on home, Terrance. Say hi to Lizzie and the boys. Thanks for busting into my place for me," she said, her voice light.

How could she make him feel good when someone had just kicked the shit out of her? He took in the snow still falling, then the open hatchback, and he closed it for her, hearing her lock the door to the shelter.

She was an amazing woman who wouldn't cower under anyone.

He was still standing there, and she walked up to him.

"It's okay, Terrance. I can see you want to do something, but you're not ready yet. Get your family settled, and get on your feet. One thing I learned long ago is if you're going to fight, you have to be ready to do it and commit to it, because once you're in it, Lord, it takes strength up here." She tapped her finger to her head. "She's trying to break me, but she won't win, because I will never give anyone that kind of power over me."

Then she walked around her car, pulled open the door, climbed inside, and started it. He stepped back on the curb, hearing the rumble as she pulled out. There was so much she was right about, but at the same time, it seemed she had a target on her.

He knew there was one thing, at least, that he could do for her: watch her back.

Sixteen

"I went ahead and replaced the faucet so you won't see a leak anymore. It looks like whoever installed it forgot to put in a seal. That's why it was leaking," Terrance said, wearing plastic booties over his boots, gripping the new black toolkit that had been waiting for him in Kent's office when he walked in for his morning update. His old tools wouldn't cut it, according to Kent, and image was everything.

"Much appreciated. What did you say your name was again, son?" asked George Schwartz, a short man—a widower in his eighties, he thought Kent had told him. A woman half his age stood out in the kitchen, dark haired, slim, neat and tidy, wearing a silky green outfit, at least two inches taller than George. Her makeup wasn't heavy, but everything about her screamed that Terrance had just stepped into a world where he knew he'd never fit.

"Terrance Mack, sir. Let me know if you have any more issues," he replied, noting that despite the high-end finishes, corners had been cut in the bathroom alone.

"You're new here, aren't you?" said George. He wore tan slacks, the kind Terrance would never be able to afford, and a dark lightweight knit. The gold ring on his pinkie finger bore a crest of some kind.

He could see the door. He would have to take only five or six steps before he could pull it open and walk out. Something about this man just made him feel so damn uncomfortable. "Yes, I just started," he said. Did the man expect him to share something else? Those carefree days of sharing with strangers were gone.

"George, I'm putting on the kettle. Did you want some tea?" the woman called out, and Terrance took that as his cue and took a step toward the door.

"Sure, Debra. Maybe this young man will join us. Terrance, is it? Come in and put your tools down." George was motioning to him from the living room, where the gas fireplace was on. The unit was a mirror image of Jennifer's penthouse apartment, the only other suite on this top floor.

"Ah, sorry, sir. I have to get back to work. Another time."

"No, no, I insist. Come on in and sit down. Leave your tools there."

He remembered a warning that morning from Kent to handle George Schwartz with kid gloves. Who the hell was he, anyways? His heart was hammering, but the man staring back at him wasn't taking no for an answer. He squeezed the handle of his toolkit and then set it down as he heard a kettle, and he wiped his sweaty palms on his heavy dark work pants before taking a step into the living room.

George stood by an easy chair and gestured to a light leather sofa. "Come on and sit down," he said.

Terrance's eyes went to the artwork on the wall. Expensive, he knew, and tasteful, maybe, though it was nothing he'd consider no matter how much money he had.

George was still standing as Terrance sat, hearing the swoosh of the leather. Then he sat in an easy chair across from him, and Debra walked in, carrying a tray with a teapot, cups, and cream and sugar.

"What would you like in your tea, Terrance?" she said as she poured three mugs. She had a nice soft voice. She poured milk in one and stirred it before taking it over to George.

"Just a little sugar, if you don't mind," he said.

"Of course." She settled a coaster on the glass sofa table in front of him with the mug of tea. Then she lifted the third mug, walked over to the other easy chair by the fireplace, and sat. She smiled brightly.

The way George was looking at him, watching him, only added to his unease. He reached for the mug and lifted it, gesturing in his awkwardness. "Thank you again."

"So you have a family, I understand?" George said.

Thud, thud. His heart slammed. Was the man angry? He didn't know what to think of his comment. Terrance's boys were quiet. He'd already warned them.

"Yes, I do." He really didn't want to share anything about his family with anyone.

"John and Greg," George said. "And you have a wife, Lizzie. You lived on the streets for how long?"

He wondered if his face paled, if everyone in the building knew the rock bottom he'd crawled from. "Too long," he replied. "I assure you I can do my job well. But, no disrespect, sir, my personal life and my family shouldn't be up for discussion."

"I have no doubt you'll do a good job," George said. "Don't be so prickly over there. Jennifer likes to say she's done her good for the year. And you're right that your personal life is just that, but when Jennifer Krause hires you, you do give over some of your freedom and rights. She expects loyalty and will point out whenever she has the chance that she saved you from disaster."

He hadn't taken a sip, maybe because of how tightly the knot squeezed in his stomach. He felt the frayed tightrope he could be walking.

"No," George continued, "I can tell by your face that all this talk of Jennifer Krause is making you uncomfortable. But she has minions who do her bidding, and she demands one hundred and fifty percent loyalty from everyone she hires. Your personal life is irrelevant to her, as are your wife and children, because you're just a stepping-stone for her. She wants something, she gets it, and she doesn't much care whom she steps on, crushes, destroys, or leaves bleeding in the wake…"

"Excuse me, Mr. Schwartz, what is this?" Terrance said. "I'm not interested in being dragged into a political suicide. Are you trying to get me to speak ill of Jennifer, of Bridgeman Towers or anyone who works here? Because I won't, if that's what this is all about. I'll say thank you for the tea, but I don't play these games. I'm well aware of how people speak, and I don't know what you're trying to get me to say about Jennifer, but I won't." He put his tea down and stood up. "I've lived on the streets with my wife and kids, and now we have a roof over our heads, and I have a job I'm good at. The only thing I want to do now is get back to work, if it's all the same to you. Thank you for the tea."

The old man smiled and gestured toward him. "Sit down, young man. Your outrage is notable—and refreshing. Seems a good many years since I've been put in my place by someone with principles."

Terrance didn't know what was coming next. Damn it!

It was as if he were suddenly playing a game without a clue what the rules were.

"Please sit," George said. "I apologize, if that will make you feel better. Jennifer will be very happy to know of your loyalty."

Terrance wondered if George or Debra could hear his heart thudding long and loud in his ears. He made himself sit back on that leather seat as he took in his tools by the door, a door he wished he were on the other side of.

"Do you know who I am, Terrance?"

He didn't want to drink the tea in front of him. He made himself shake his head and said, "George Schwartz. You own the penthouse suite across from Jennifer Krause, who's the owner of Bridgeman Towers."

The man smiled again, not the kind of smile that eased Terrance in any way. He steepled his hands in front of him. Then there was Debra, who he could feel watching him intently. What the hell was her story? By the massive diamond on her finger, she was married. To George? He didn't know.

"Let me tell you a story, young man, about who really runs things," George said. "Jennifer owns shares in Bridgeman, which is part of a larger company owned by another shell company inside another shell company. When I fund something, it's to benefit me. Bridgeman was funded by me. I'm an investor. Some people call me a philanthropist. I fund many global organizations. I made my money early on by buying failing companies and dismantling them. I guess you can say I made destroying something and building it back up in my image my life's work. Isn't that right, Debra?"

Debra was no longer smiling as she held the mug of tea, watching Terrance like someone who didn't have a care in the world. "Oh, George, that was when you were younger and operated on emotion. You're actually a lot more careful now that you're more interested in being behind the scenes, shaping policies. Ignore what my husband has said, Terrance. He likes to really test people's characters."

Terrance didn't know what to do with his hands, so he linked them together and tried to wrap his head around what George Schwartz had said. So he was the boss. Now Terrance had more questions than answers—namely, what did he want with him?

"You lost your home," George said. "The contractor you worked for closed up shop one day, took all the money, and disappeared. You hired a lawyer who took what you had left only to tell you you'd never see the money you were owed. The contractor had done this before, two hundred and thirty-five times before, in fact. He pockets the wealth, starts up somewhere else, and steals more. In the developments he builds, problems are suddenly found, but a contractor who's gone out of business can't be sued. He uses that loophole to further screw people. He starts a new company and does the same thing again.

"What was his name, Mike Emerson? I can tell by your face that I've hit a nerve. You know, Mike has property in the Caymans, one of the best tax shelters around. He's amassed over two hundred million in his shell game, yet your family had to sleep in a tent, freezing, having lost everything because this man got away with taking it. How many other families has he done this to? His trail of destruction is wide, yet you'll never get justice because he's too wealthy now, and the policies and legislation protect him. So how much would you like to get back at him?"

There it was, that sick feeling again, along with anger at having allowed himself to trust in a system that hadn't protected him. He reached for the now cooled tea, lifted it and took a big swallow, and then put it down.

"Mr. Schwartz, I really would appreciate your letting me know if I can fix anything else around here, if there are any more problems, but I do really need to get back to work," he said, then stood up.

George was watching him, as was Debra, who he now knew was his wife. He wondered why Kent had said he was widowed.

"You know what, son?" George said. "I can see you're angry, but you're holding your cards close to your chest. I like that."

Terrance nodded to him, then glanced over to Debra and said, "Thank you for the tea, ma'am." He made himself walk over to the door and reached down to pick up his toolkit.

"A man who thinks first rather than speaking out in anger is a man who will go far and a man to be wary of. I've made it my life to read people. You'll go far, Terrance. When you're ready, you come and see me."

Terrance had his hand on the doorknob. He glanced back over to the man who seemed to know every one of his secrets. "I'm just trying to do my job, Mr. Schwartz, and get back on my feet."

George met his stare. "You're a smart man, Terrance Mack, exactly the kind of man people can relate to and will vote for. An opening will be coming up in the city council. It's a foot in the door. Next year, the current mayor is going to have some financial issues or a personal crisis, and an early election is going to be called. Six key states have senators who are likely serving their last years, and their sons are slated to inherit their positions in all but one. Then there are the governors who will be replaced in the next three years."

The knot in his stomach tightened, and he knew he made a face. "Who are you?"

The man didn't stand up. "We're leaving on Friday for our place in Florida. You'll let me know if you need anything before then? Take care of your family, Terrance."

And that was it. He knew he was being dismissed, so he pulled open the door and stepped out, then pulled the door closed.

As he started to the elevator, he glanced back at the door to the penthouse. Whoever this man was, really was, he could see to it that Terrance never worked again. He held the kind of power no man should ever have the right to.

The elevator dinged, and when it slid open, there was Jennifer. She stepped out and walked past him, letting her gaze run down over him, and he could feel her distaste for him. Then she snapped her fingers and turned back to him before he could step into the elevator.

"You're the maintenance guy. What was your name again?"

His heart thudded. "Terrance."

She nodded. "Right, Terrance. You looked after George?"

He slapped his hand to the door of the elevator so it wouldn't close. "Yes, just a missing faucet seal. All taken care of."

She didn't smile as she flicked her gaze to the closed double doors of George Schwartz's unit. She let her gaze linger, then turned and started walking away. So that was it, dismissed again. He went to step into the elevator.

"Oh, Terrance, in half an hour I want you to come up for a meeting," she said.

He was still holding the door. "You mean up here or in Kent's office?"

She had her key in the door, then turned back to him. "My place, half an hour. Don't be late." Then she opened her door, stepped inside, and closed it.

When the elevator buzzed, he stepped inside and let it close, not looking up at the security camera. He couldn't shake the feeling that he was stepping from one viper's nest into another.

Seventeen

Terrance glanced at his watch. He still had five minutes until he was supposed to be knocking on Jennifer's door. As the elevator dinged and opened, his heart thudded and his palms were sweating. He was too early! But if he went back down, he would be late, so he stepped out of the elevator, seeing his image in the mirror, his gray shirt and heavy workpants.

"Where is your human decency? How could you?"

He knew that voice. At the door to the penthouse was Misty, wearing an old wool coat, and Jennifer, wearing a silky white shirt and pants, her arms crossed. He thought she had a few inches on her sister. Damn, he still couldn't believe they were related.

"How did you get in here?" Jennifer said. They were family, but he could hear not an ounce of caring in her tone.

"You mean how did I get past your building security when you gave them my photo and instructed them to keep me out, telling them to call the police if necessary?

Message received. They didn't let me in, but I know more than one way to get where I'm going."

Misty was angry—no, furious. Terrance took a step closer despite the fact that Kenny's reminder was always on his mind. He was supposed to stay out of Jennifer and Misty's business, but now it was happening right in front of him.

"So is that why you're here, to cry and whine to me about how unfairly you're being treated?" Jennifer said. "Well, grow the fuck up, because I will never apologize for anything, and I will not be intimidated by you. Seriously, look at yourself."

Terrance couldn't imagine how a sister could look at her own blood with that kind of disgust. What had happened? As he took another step, he felt the underlying tension that simmered between the sisters.

"You're disgusting," Jennifer continued. "You look like those pathetic losers you're always giving handouts to. You even smell like them." She wrinkled her nose.

Terrance told himself he shouldn't take another step, but this cruelty was too much for him.

"Why do you do this?" Misty said. "I don't understand why you want my building— mine! I've stayed out of your business. You have all this, yet you're responsible for those people having nothing. I mean, who did you pay off to get this city to suddenly go back on its agreement? You tossed those people out. This was supposed to be low-cost housing for them. It was in that proposal to city council.

"It would have benefited the community, cleaned up the streets, and gotten rid of that rat-infested moldy building, replacing it with something decent and clean and fixing everything that was wrong, the corroded pipes, the faulty wiring. Yet instead you tore it down, and the people fought back because they knew what the folks representing them refused to see, which was that it would become just another place for the rich man, one less place for those folks. So you're damn right I'm looking after them, doing what I can."

Jennifer started laughing. The elevator dinged behind him, and he turned back to see Clark, the security guard, stepping off. Terrance took another step closer until both women were staring right at him.

Misty let out a sigh of frustration, and he didn't miss the lingering sadness in her eyes. She was being kicked over and over, but she was refusing to go down. Damn, did he admire her and despise her sister.

"You okay?" he said as he stepped closer. He couldn't not ask, yet he didn't have to look over to Jennifer to know he wasn't supposed to have done so.

"I'm fine, Terrance," Misty said. Then she looked past him, and Clark was right there. He wondered whether he was going to put his hand on her.

"So you called for security, did you?" Misty said. "Pathetic, Jennifer. You always did have someone fighting your battles. Wasn't that what you said, that you'd be bigger and stronger and would crush anyone who got in your way? What happened to you? Dad would roll over in his grave if he could see what you turned into—one of them, the same ones who took everything we had."

"Dad was a fool," Jennifer cut in, her arms crossed. By the way she leaned in, he wondered whether she hated her father too.

"He was our father, Jennifer, and he did his best. Does it make you feel better, being the big man, able to destroy people, to take from them? My place wasn't much, but it was a warm place for people to go, to put food in their bellies. You've sent bylaw officers, sent thugs to bust lights and cause a disturbance and blame it on the people I'm helping. You've lied, you've cheated…"

"Oh, blah, blah, blah, here we go again about how I'm stealing from the poor. I'll tell you what I'm doing: making sure I will never be as pathetic as you, Dad, or Mom. They had no backbone. They allowed someone to walk into our house and take what they wanted because they could. I swore no one would take from me ever again. Instead I'd be the one doing the taking.

"You think you're helping those pathetic souls? You're not helping them; you're enabling them. If they weren't so gutless, they'd have figured out a way to pull themselves up and out of the gutter. I'm no bleeding heart. But you know what? They should thank me for putting them out of the misery of going along with their pathetic existence, living off welfare and food stamps, where their biggest accomplishment is buying cheap gin to drown their sorrows. Nope, I can't stand that or them. The best thing would be for every one of them to OD in the streets. It would make it so much easier—"

The slap shut Jennifer up. Terrance stared at the red handprint on her face. He'd never expected Misty to hit her so hard. The silence was deafening, and the shock on Jennifer's face had his heart hammering.

"Get her out of here and toss her in the streets," Jennifer bit out to Clark, who now had his hand on Misty's shoulder. She shrugged him off, and Terrance took a step forward again, his hands fisted as he faced Jennifer, but he felt a hand on his arm.

"Terrance, it's fine. I'm leaving," Misty said.

"You going to be okay?" he finally asked as he looked back to her. Clark showed nothing in his expression, but Terrance could see he'd do exactly what Jennifer ordered.

"She's fine," Jennifer said. "You remember who you work for, or do you want to join her?"

"Jennifer," came a deep male voice, and Terrance turned to see Kenny stepping off the elevator and walking their way. "What's going on here?" He was looking at Jennifer, then dragged his gaze over to Misty.

"Nothing," Misty said. "Just setting some ground rules with my sister."

"You've set nothing," Jennifer replied. "You just drag your sorry ass out of here and back to that riffraff scum. Deliver your sandwiches from the back of your car, and when the wrecking ball and bulldozer show up to tear down your building, I'll be right there in the front row, watching, taking the first swing to bring it down. I'll leave it as a parking lot just so you can't have it." Jennifer leaned in, spiteful, spitting, angry. Damn, why did she hate Misty so much?

"Well, you just try doing that," Misty said. "It ain't going to be as easy as you think, Jennifer. I will not go down without a fight. I sleep well at night when I close my eyes, but how well do you sleep? Do you hear the cries of the people you've stolen from? Do you feel their pain, or do you drown it in pills and whiskey, telling yourself it's okay because of the color of your skin? You should be ashamed to be a black woman, Jennifer, for what you're doing to your own people…"

"Get out!" Jennifer yelled, her hands fisted.

Clark reached for her arm. "Let's go. Come on, Misty," he said.

Kenny stepped around them as Misty shrugged off Clark's hand and started to the elevator. Terrance wished he could leave with her, but when he went to turn, Kenny set a hand on his arm and just shook his head.

"My people?" Jennifer called out. "They're not my people. They're nobodies."

The elevator dinged, and Misty looked back as Clark held the door open, waiting for her to step on. "You just keep telling yourself that, but you sold your soul, Jennifer. You can take my money, my property, the roof over my head, my car, and you can dry up any income I have, but you won't win—because my soul isn't for sale. There are worse things than death, but I'm sure you already know that."

Then Misty stepped into the elevator.

Terrance took in the unsettled rage in the face of a woman it now sickened him to be around.

She blew out a breath and pasted a smile on her face. "Well, sorry about that. Kenny, just give me a minute with, ah…" She actually snapped her fingers.

Terrance had to remind himself he was one step from being out the door and back on the street as he said, "Terrance. You asked me to come up in half an hour for a meeting."

How the hell had he gotten his voice that calm?

She shut her eyes and touched her forehead as if trying to pull herself together, then clapped her hands. She was the ugliest woman he'd ever seen even though her image was the opposite.

"Right, it was about your children," she said. "I want you to be clear on the rules. They have to use the back door and can't be seen by the residents here. I don't want to have them playing on the stairs and creating a ruckus. You may have them, but I don't want to see or hear them."

He had to fight the urge to roll his shoulders and tell her his children hadn't stepped out of line. "With all due respect, my sons are aware of your rules and have been respectful."

He felt a hand on his shoulder, maybe because Kenny sensed he wasn't going to let Jennifer grind his children into the ground.

"Great to see you again, Terrance," Kenny said. "You should check in with Kent. Jennifer, I think we have a few things to go over…"

Jennifer had turned and was now walking away inside her penthouse. Kenny stepped into the open doorway and glanced back to him. Like, what the hell was that about?

"Careful, Terrance," he said. "Be smart. Jennifer isn't Misty."

He had so much he wanted to add, but the warning that stared back at him had him backing up and lifting his hands in surrender. "Yeah, I got that."

Kenny had his hand on the door. He jutted his chin. "It'll blow over in a few days. Just keep your head down. Best to stay off her radar." Then he closed it.

Terrance took a step toward the elevator, but at the end of the hall, he took in the open door of the other penthouse suite. George Schwartz was standing there, his expression unreadable. Then he stepped back inside and closed the door without saying one word to Terrance.

He really did feel as if he were in the middle of a game without knowing the rules or exactly who the players were.

Eighteen

"This is a wonderful dinner," Terrance said as he took in the pot roast. His boys were finishing their plates, and he knew the leftovers would become sandwiches. "You know, I've never been a praying man, but I remember a time when dinner was rushed, and I never appreciated what we had."

Lizzie had her dark hair pulled back, wearing a burgundy sweatshirt. "I guess that would make two of us. Are you two done?" she said to the boys as John got up to the leave the table, his plate still there. "Clean up after yourselves, dishes in the dishwasher."

She didn't pull her gaze from the boys until they had left the table and were in the kitchen, the dishwasher open, loading their dishes. She sat there for another second in quiet, and something about her told him she had something on her mind.

"The boys couldn't get in the back door this afternoon after school," she said. "John lost the key. He said they walked around to the front and were questioned by one of the security guys, and then some fancy woman named Ms.

Krause asked them what they wanted. John said he told her they lived here and were just coming home from school. He told Greg not to say anything, but Greg said their dad is Terrance Mack, the maintenance manager, very important. He said Ms. Krause yelled at them and told them never to walk in the front door of her building again or their dad would be fired. She scared them. John grabbed Greg and told him to be quiet. He was pretty scared. He didn't tell me right away. I know he was talking about Jennifer Krause. You mentioned her. John said the pocket he put his key in has a hole."

Terrance shut his eyes. Too much of his day was now making sense. He had his elbows resting on the table and shut his eyes for a second, then sighed. "Well, she did come at me today with a warning about the boys. I thought she was just stirring up trouble. I'll talk to the boys. They cannot come in the front door again, Lizzie."

She only nodded, and he really looked at her, seeing how unusually tired she still seemed.

"I'll get another key cut, but how about you walk with them for the next little bit? I don't think either of us is ready to be back on the street. I need to put some money away for us, and then I can look for something else. Misty was here, and she and Jennifer really had it out. I know you want me not to get involved, but I don't think I can do that. Jennifer managed to get her hands on Misty's building, the one that saved us, and she plans to have it taken down. I don't know why she hates her sister so much…"

He stopped talking because he could see how uneasy his wife was. She turned from him and stared out to the living room, thinking, considering. He had once known what dark thoughts plagued her, but now he had no idea.

"So a woman who has everything and takes from everyone is trying to destroy a woman who gives to everyone, who feeds the homeless and does something no one else will." She flicked her gaze to him. "If you're going to help her, don't do it here. You're right that we can't move right now, and she would likely toss us out without a second thought. I'm going to get a job while the boys are in school, too. I won't leave it all to you to fix."

She slid off her chair and reached for the casserole dish, the leftover potatoes, then looked at him. "I know I said you can't help Misty, but if something happens again, I know how it feels when people are too afraid to speak up. I know you, Terrance, so whatever you're going to do, be smart."

He sat back in his chair, looking at his wife. He heard a knock at the door and didn't miss the fear in her face. He stood up, touched her arm, and said, "I'll get it." Then he gestured to the boys in the living room, the TV on, and said, "Go to your room."

He waited only a second as his boys left before he opened the door to see a man he'd never expected, Kenny. He was in a leather coat, tall, a big man.

"You have a minute, Terrance? I wanted to talk with you about earlier."

Terrance glanced down the hall, then stepped back. "Sure, come on in."

Kenny nodded and stepped inside, his gaze going right to Lizzie in the kitchen.

"Hi, Kenny. Nice to see you again," she said.

Terrance closed the door and gestured to the table. "Do you want to come in and sit down?"

Kenny shook his head and glanced over to his wife again, and maybe she knew he wanted to talk alone, as she closed up the dishwasher and said, "I'll give you two some privacy." Then she strode out and down the hall.

It was quiet. Terrance listened to the bedroom door close.

"Okay, so what is this, another warning from Jennifer?" he said. "Maybe you want to explain to me the relationship you have to Jennifer and Misty. You were at the shelter with Misty, but here you are, always with Jennifer. I can piece a lot together, but I can't help shaking this feeling that I'm a pawn in some game."

Kenny didn't smile, only glanced away as if thinking. "Jennifer takes, and Misty gives. You already know they're sisters, yet one would kill the other and probably not even lose sleep over it. Some would say that makes her evil or sociopathic. She builds and steals and makes more and more. Her growing hatred for Misty is out of control and clouds her judgement in everything.

"She finally managed to get her hands on Misty's building, and I only found out this morning. When Jennifer is working on something, she gets all happy and only lets teasing bits of information out. I've learned to take cover then, because it means she's going to pull the rug out from under someone. She doesn't play by the rules society is supposed to play by. She makes up her own rules and walks in the shadows. She's not the kind of person who needs to like the woman looking back at her in the mirror."

He stared at Kenny and shrugged. "You think I haven't figured that out? So answer me this: Misty and Jennifer, how long have you known them?" He pulled his arms over his chest, wondering if Kenny would answer.

"I always knew Jennifer. We dated when we were young. Then she married someone else, and so did I. I went through the police academy, while she was moving in circles I never would. She called me over the years. I was divorced, and she married two more times. Long story short, I never knew she had a sister. When she took down this building, I remember listening to her and how happy it made her to displace those she called 'wasted people breathing up air they have no right to.'

"I thought she was joking, but she took the city's money and funneled it to her organization. It was meant to go toward rebuilding this place into something new and livable, but instead she did what too many in this country do. She pre-sold the units to investors who just park their money, taking tax write-offs. The city and councilors have done this so many times that there seems to be a script to manage the outrage. No investigations are done, or at least no meaningful ones. The councilors and the right city officials get perks, kickbacks, and everyone is onto something new tomorrow.

"But one day a spitfire showed up to challenge Jennifer, and she wouldn't back down like everyone else. I learned she was her sister. I paid a visit to Misty, who still to this day doesn't trash-talk her sister, although she has every right. Misty is a very good woman, and Jennifer is very confused. I'm not a good person, Terrance. I've done things I wish I could undo. Maybe the little I can do for Misty is my way of trying to make it right for a woman I can't help but love."

In the ensuing silence, Kenny pulled his hands from his pockets and looked down. Terrance could see he was getting ready to leave.

"Once, I thought I could be the one to stop Jennifer…" He shook his head and glanced back up. "You have something I admire. If you fight Jennifer, someone who's been playing this game for a long time, you need to be smart and patient and have a plan. She has friends in places you wouldn't expect. She has people who will sell you and your children out. I know you talked to George, but I'm going to say this anyway: They are both snakes, one deadlier than the other. Keep your eyes open and your ears to the ground. Remember that old saying: Keep your friends close but your enemies closer."

Then he reached around for the door and pulled it open. When he looked back, Terrance thought he was going to say something, but he didn't. He started walking down the hall.

Terrance closed the door just as his wife appeared, wide eyed, around the corner.

"What was that about?" she said.

He stepped away from the door and took in this place, their refuge for the moment. "A warning, I think, and a confirmation."

"Of what?"

He hesitated only a second before saying, "That there's only one choice. I'm getting us back on our feet, but I have no intention of selling my soul to the devil."

CHAPTER
Nineteen

Jennifer, George, Kenny.

Their names kept going through his head as he finished checking another empty and unused suite. He stared at his list of all the presold units that had never been occupied, and he ached for a moment as he thought of everyone who was living on the streets.

The elevator dinged, and he pulled at his coat and stepped out, taking in Clark alone behind the security desk. The man looked up but said nothing, then glanced back down, and something in that one look bothered Terrance in ways he couldn't have explained.

"Terrance, young man. You're just who I'm looking for."

He turned to see the old guy, George Schwartz, with his much younger wife, both wearing heavy overcoats, having stepped off the elevator. The man was smiling and wore a gray dress hat, and all Terrance could think as he stared at the two of them was that George was much shorter than his wife. The man had a cane, but he didn't think he needed it.

Terrance realized he'd stepped into a game the moment he'd taken the job in this building. He wondered if everyone who worked there had figured out the same thing.

"Mr. Schwartz, how is everything?" he said. "Any more problems in your unit?"

George gestured toward him, and he noticed a ring on his finger. "Oh, everything is fine up there. Wondering if you have a moment to walk with us. Debra, do you want to see that the car is brought around?"

He still wondered about the marriage, the relationship.

Debra said only, "Of course," before walking over to Clark at the desk.

Terrance turned back to George, who was holding that cane and watching him as if trying to understand who he was and what he was thinking. Something about the way he looked at him made him uneasy.

"Let's step outside," George said. "There's something about Montana winters that I love." He gestured toward the door, and Terrance started walking and pushed it open, then held it for the old man.

The pavers out front were perfectly cleared, and at least the snow had stopped for now. He waited for the old man to walk out and then fell in beside him, letting the door swing closed.

"So your family is comfortable?" George asked.

Unease tightened in Terrance's chest. "Yes, we're quite comfortable."

George gestured with his cane as a black luxury town car pulled up. "Ride with me. It will give me a chance to talk with you."

The driver stepped out and opened the back door. Terrance took in the luxury as the old man waited for him.

"Well, come on, son," he said.

"What about your wife?" Terrance gestured back to the building, but he didn't see Debra.

"Oh, this is just for you and me," George said, then slid in the car.

The driver walked around to the other side and pulled open the door. Terrance wanted to say no, and it was on the edge of his tongue as he took in the building again, feeling the cold, knowing he was still under the mercy of someone who could have them tossed out again. But he made himself take one step and then another and slide past the door the driver was holding open, into the backseat beside George. The door closed, and the air was warm.

"You have a way about you, Terrance. You keep your head down and have skillful hands." George hadn't bothered with his seatbelt. He lifted his hand when the driver climbed behind the wheel and said, "Lawrence, take us over to the project."

"Of course, Mr. Schwartz."

The car pulled out into traffic. Terrance knew he should ask what the project was.

"You don't talk much," George continued. "I like that. Principled, too. Been a long time since someone turned me down about anything. Usually, everyone is trying to get close to me, get something from me. So what is it that you desire, Terrance, that you're working for? Everyone has a big picture."

Terrance took in the road and the smooth ride, the streets he would have been walking now. "You asking me to tell you my hopes and dreams? Sorry, Mr. Schwartz, and no disrespect, but I'm not sure how that's any of your business. I don't know you. But I do work hard, and I'm trying to put enough away so that my family never ends up with nothing again. I take it one day at a time, but for me, the future is about securing something stable for my kids and my wife."

He couldn't have explained it to anyone, but he didn't like this man poking into his personal life. George only laughed softly as the driver slowed, and Terrance took in the concrete lot filled with garbage and junk, remembering their first night at the camp, which he'd spent with a group of people who had put him right in the path of Misty, the shelter, and the job he had now.

"You know any of those folks in there?" George gestured out the window, and the car slowed.

Terrance took in the bundled-up people, the misfits he'd once thought were teens who'd picked the streets over a home in the system. "You know, Mr. Schwartz, the first night we came here, we camped with those folks, a mix of good and bad, and every one of them had a sad story about how they'd got there. How many do you think lived in the very building I now work in before it was torn down and turned into something they could never afford? There are some kids in there, too, and they choose this life because it's safer than a system of foster homes that has never protected them. A few people out there would kill these people, so it's a wonder they wake up every morning without giving up."

The old man was looking at him, then gestured again. "Keep going," he said to the driver, who pulled away and went around another block.

Terrance spotted Misty in her old car, the hatchback open and some of the homeless beside her—handing out food, he thought.

"You know the story of Jennifer and Misty," George said.

Terrance couldn't pull his gaze from the old man.

"Well, of course you do," he continued. "Kenny

brought you in, and he's never been known for discretion. Unfortunately for him, he has a conscience, but I wonder if Jennifer ever had one. You care for Misty, don't you?" George didn't look at him, and he couldn't shake the feeling that this was all some test.

"She saved me and my family. Of course I do. So why is it that Jennifer took her building from her and hates her so much? Is she really going to bulldoze a place that's a refuge for so many? And how does she have the power to have Misty's place shut down? A closure from the city? I just don't understand."

The car pulled around the block and parked in front of the building in question, Misty's, with the padlock still on there and closure papers taped across it.

"Jennifer hates the weak, as she puts it," George said, "all those lost souls that Misty is trying to save. If you look back, I think Misty has done that her whole life for Jennifer. Sometimes I think some people are born without a soul."

That was the strangest thing he'd ever heard someone say, and he wondered if his face showed what he was thinking.

George reached over and patted his arm. "Oh, I've lived a long time and run in a circle of people who aren't like you, Terrance. Wealth, privilege, family, money, power, greed… Idealism is something I rarely see anymore. Instead, it's a game. We drive past a building and see an eyesore, a rundown, broken-down place, and we see the people there as useless eaters, as Jennifer calls them. What makes her happy is being able to make a place her project, tossing people out onto the streets and tearing it down.

"She gets there by owning the political wing, right down to the councilors. She makes the calls and knows the laws so she can manipulate the entire project to her benefit and pocket all the profits. You know how it's done? First budgets are created at the federal and state levels, billions and trillions itemized in a huge budget that no one ever questions, and if someone does, that person suddenly finds himself under investigation for something.

"Let's take last year's budget to upgrade the routers in the libraries across the country to increase the capacity. It was 28 million, which came down to roughly $28,600 per router. Yes, I can tell by your expression that it took you only a few seconds to see that doesn't add up."

Terrance blinked. "We're talking a cheap internet router—a few hundred, maybe, or a thousand if someone is being fleeced." But the old man was still smiling, and it left Terrance with a sick feeling in his stomach. "You're serious, aren't you?"

"Young man, I'm quite serious. I don't have the temperament to kid around, as you call it."

Terrance had to pull in a breath. He took in the old building, feeling the weight of what this man was saying. "So what happened to all the money? That's the taxpayers' money, state and federal…"

"I see you have a lot of questions. Ask yourself this. Who owns the telecommunications company that's providing the routers? How many of them were actually installed? Then look at who owns the parent company of that telecommunications company, which maybe owns many more big companies. That parent company is owned by a foundation, a charitable one with a tax-free status. Then look at the shareholders of the company, a few key politicians who ensure the right legislation is passed and control where the contracts go for the budgets they create every year.

"You know who funds all of this, the building you work in, the routers that were installed in likely only half of the libraries? It was funded entirely on the backs of the middle class, all those taxes that keep going up and up. And the foundation those millions and millions are funneled through paid roughly ninety-three dollars in taxes last year because of the loopholes and legislation created for them. Jennifer made a few calls to our corrupt city council to shut Misty down, and now she owns this building too."

Terrance realized he was serious. Anger burned inside him. "That's not legal. You can't just take someone's property from her." He knew it had come out quite sharply.

"The law has nothing to do with it. Laws apply only to you and the everyday people who pay for everything here. People like me and Jennifer, the law doesn't apply to us. We put people in office to write it, and if we want someone's property, we take it."

Terrance let out a rough rude sound. "Unbelievable," he said under his breath.

"Oh no, it's very believable. Look, Terrance, I don't often do this, but as I said to you earlier, there's an opening coming up with the council here. I want to put your name in. I will ask only once."

George said nothing else, and Terrance felt the seconds ticking.

"And why would you do that?" he finally said.

The old man was gripping his cane in front of him, and his hard, chiseled expression seemed almost stonelike. "You want to help Misty? You want to do something to help those miscreants out there? You know there's a multi-million-dollar budget created every year to help the homeless, but less than one percent ever reaches them. That's where you change things. That's where you put a stop to the Jennifers who steal and take and divert money. That's how you put a stop to the corruption, by being the one voice who can't be bought, or threatened, or coerced. It takes a strong man to stand up. Do you think you're up to it, Terrance?"

Why was it that it sounded too good to be true?

"And what's in this for you?"

George smiled. "You'll remember who helped you."

Terrance said nothing at first, just stared at the old man. How old was he? The shrewdness oozed from him. "I still have to be voted in. People don't know me."

"You leave all that to me. I'll let you out here."

Terrance stepped out of the vehicle and closed the door behind him, and the car pulled away. He stepped up on the curb, into the snow on a sidewalk that hadn't been shoveled. And he couldn't shake the feeling that whatever he'd just agreed to, he'd made a deal with the devil.

Twenty

He heard the door and the footsteps as he waited in the dim room, lit only by the mesh-covered windows in the kitchen. The power had been turned off, and his breath fogged in front of him from the winter cold. No power, no heat. He took in the old tables as he stepped out into the open.

"I got your message," Kenny said, striding toward him. "You bust the padlock on the front door?" He wore a dark knit hat and heavy coat, and it looked like he hadn't shaved that day. Something about his expression made Terrance wonder what side of everything he was on.

His breath fogged again, and he kept his hands shoved in his pockets. "Didn't take much. I see someone had the power shut off in here. So how soon is it before the demolition crews show up?"

The man stopped about ten feet from him, fidgeting, and gave his head a shake with an odd smile. Maybe no one knew where Kenny stood—not even Kenny himself.

"No idea," he said. "Could be days, weeks…" He lifted his hands and shrugged. Terrance had to remind himself that for some reason, Misty trusted this man, yet something about him still didn't sit right.

"So who on the council is in the pocket of Jennifer Krause?"

Kenny didn't pull his gaze, and Terrance could almost see the man thinking, maybe trying to figure out why he had left a message for him. He wanted to list off the names he'd learned: MacGuire, Talbert, Gibbs, Dumont.

"There's something different about you today, Terrance," Kenny said, "and I can't help thinking you're looking to become a problem. Are you? You haven't worked that long. Would be a shame to have you suddenly back on the outside, looking in."

There it was, something Terrance had known was there inside him. The mask had dropped. Kenny stepped back and looked away.

"Only a man who's desperate would threaten another man," Terrance said. "Don't threaten me or my family. I won't be bullied. It's a simple question, and you still haven't answered. You should know that George Schwartz has dangled a council position in front of me. Apparently, Dumont had a sudden problem come up. Someone found out he has a fondness for younger women, much younger women. So instead of fighting it, he's resigned. Schwartz wants me in that position, and according to him, he has the means to ensure I step right in. How, I'm not sure, but I'm not stupid. I didn't go to college, but I have a pretty good idea it involves a phone call to the right person and maybe a favor called in. My guess is that the dirt on Dumont likely arrived by email, photos and videos."

"So is that why you wanted me to meet you down here, because you're taking Frank Dumont's position?" Kenny said. "You already know Dumont is Jennifer's contact here, but not her only one. She has others in other states."

He fisted his hands, because he hadn't known that part. So much about Jennifer Krause was a mystery to him, but there was something suspicious in how Dumont's secrets had suddenly been exposed, and Terrance doubted he would ever get the real reason behind the story and why Dumont had to go. Schwartz had left a manilla envelope for him at the front desk containing details on every person in the political landscape of the county, right up to the state governor. Then there was Kenny.

"Will I have a problem with Jennifer now?" Terrance said. "How long do you think it will be before she's gunning for me or showing up, demanding something from me?"

Kenny pulled his hand over his face and shook his head. "You sure you want to get into that? Because there really is something to be said for politics being a dirty game. That's all it is. You planning on leaving your job, moving out? Because she'll expect something from you. She never does anything for anyone without expecting something in return, and in her mind, she did you a favor, giving you and your family a roof over your heads.

"She'll have kept track of everything. Even though you were hired to do a job, which you did, she won't see any of that. She'll have someone itemize every advance, all the food that was given to you to get you started, even the furnished suite, and she'll expect repayment—and it won't be anything you can afford. She'll expect you to do every-thing for her, everything she asks, without question.

"Right now, this here…" Kenney flicked his hand and circled it in the air, then looked up to the stained, dated ceiling. "She'll insist you prove your loyalty, and that will mean taking this building down and seeing to it that any obstacles are dealt with, including Misty. Are you prepared for that?"

Terrance didn't understand how Kenny could be with a woman like Jennifer and pretend to care for Misty. "Is that what she's insisted of you? When I first stepped in here, you were acting as a bodyguard for Misty. Then those cops busted in and gave me a beating. You gave me a story to go along with and made sure I would stay in line at the hospital. I was supposed to just swallow it. You told me you don't know what Jennifer is up to or what she plans to do next in gunning for Misty. But I have a hard time believing that. You want to tell me what George has on you?"

There it was, a flicker in his blue eyes as they landed on him. Terrance knew Kenny was someone with a lot of buried skeletons.

"Now why would you ask me that?" Kenny took a step toward him. He was bigger than Terrance, but there was no way he would allow himself to be intimidated.

"You know, I can't help wondering what George Schwartz wants with me," Terrance said, "offering me a council position just like that. For whatever reason, he can have me, a nobody, walking in there and becoming the new councilman on the block just like that, no vote, nothing. But I'll owe him, and one day I'm sure he'll come to collect.

"How many people do you think Schwartz has something on, hundreds, thousands? When a man like him hands over information on the people who run things in this town—and every one of them has done something, and Schwartz has the evidence—it must come down to money, a lot of money. I never in a million years would have expected so many men and even women to have done inappropriate things with kids.

"Then there's the budget, all the tax dollars paid by people like you and me, with additional federal grants and donations, diverted to projects funded by shell companies, whose directors are paid—legitimately, mind you—because of how the contracts are awarded. I guess I never gave it much thought, where all the taxes I paid were going. You just shut it off, driving down a road filled with potholes that never seem to get filled even though the money is there for infrastructure, programs, labor costs, equipment purchases, insurance for God knows what, and enormous administration expenses.

"When you think of all the departments that need funding to run the city, how does a mayor have a ten-acre recreational property in Wyoming paid for by taxpayers? I could go on, but I can tell by your face that you know what I'm talking about. There are photos and emails to prove it all. Then there was you, who buried evidence of missing kids. Money misappropriation is bad, and it makes me downright furious, but what makes me absolutely ill and terrified in a way I've never been was seeing how that evidence went missing.

"Forty-six Haitian kids, here one day and then gone. There was an email from a senator here, organizing the process of bringing them in because they were orphaned. He had permission from the Haitian president because he promised to find them homes in the foster system to start, but then they just disappeared. And what did you say in the email to Senator Pauley? 'Don't worry. No one will be looking for them.' Yet there were photos of the senator with those kids." He gestured toward Kenny, seeing the way his jaw tightened, a muscle twitching.

Kenny shook his head. "You're right about one thing: George has something on everyone. So what did he give you on me, photos, emails, bank accounts?"

Terrance's heart thudded, and he had to remind himself to breathe. "As I said, George gave me something on everyone. My surprise was about what he gave me on you. So again, why did you do it? And why Misty?"

Kenny dragged his hand over his head. "I'm not the same person I used to be. Yes, I did some bad things. Being a cop, you'll find that people who have money, status, and power in politics always come calling. You get invited to parties, to the inner circle, if they like you. Being a cop anywhere is one of the lowest and shittiest-paying jobs, and it comes with a ton of headaches. I'm not a bad person, but I did bad things.

"You want to know what happened to those kids?" He shrugged. "So would I. From the little digging I did, I realized they were trafficked along with hundreds of thousands, and the senator was part of it but not the head of it. I don't even know how many are involved, but there are a lot. I also realized I wasn't the only one on the force doing bad things. A cop who's bad needs to be good at it so there's no way a good cop can see what he's doing. I didn't know if the chief of police, the sergeant, or the beat cops were owned. No one was looking for the kids.

"I made sure the records from the bus company disappeared because I was told to make sure there was no trail, and the next day there was a deposit for fifty-five thousand dollars in my account. Maybe in my naïveté I thought it was a one-time thing, but it wasn't. It happened overnight. You do one thing, and they own you after that. Pretty soon I wasn't sleeping because I realized something truly evil was going on in this world, yet no one could see it. But I saw it, and one day I had enough. Maybe doing what I can for Misty is the only way I can think to make right everything I've done. Sure, I did some good things as a cop, but I also used that badge to make evidence disappear, to do things that went against what a cop is supposed to do. George will own you now."

Terrance had to look away, maybe because he knew he'd never like Kenny. "I never said I was taking the position."

Kenny narrowed his eyes. "You said he gave you evidence. You're going to say no to George? It doesn't work that way with a man like him. You have no idea who he is. As soon as he has his sights set on you, he owns you." Kenny took a step toward him, then glanced over to the door, but there was no one there. It was quiet, and Terrance thought he heard the wind picking up outside.

"I figured," Terrance said, "but the thing is that I can't be bought. Maybe I considered taking the position for a second because then I could help Misty. But selling my soul isn't going to help her, because how many more will it hurt?"

"He'll break you."

Terrance knew that should have scared him. "He can try, but he can succeed only if I fear him, and I won't give him that."

It was quiet for a moment.

"I can't protect you."

Maybe he hadn't expected that. "I wouldn't ask you to. Misty is going to lose this." Terrance felt Kenny watching him.

"You could save it for her."

He knew what Kenny was saying, but he only shook his head. "Not this way, I can't. I'd do anything for her, but I will not owe anyone or sell my soul."

Kenny pulled in a deep breath and let it out. "I'm going to head out." He took a step and then glanced back. "I envy you, Terrance. If I had a chance to go back and not do it again, I like to think I'd say no, but remembering who I was then, I know I would have done exactly the same thing. I was unhappy, miserable, and was being screwed over by my first lying, cheating wife. I think they knew that. A man full of hate and anger, wanting to hurt others like I was hurting."

Kenny shook his head and looked away, then started walking to the door. "When you tell George," he called out over his shoulder, "don't let the old man fool you when he smiles and says not to worry about it. Protect your family, your boys, because he'll come at you again, and next time, he'll try to hurt you."

Terrance thought he was going to say something else, but he just shook his head and stepped out, and the door closed behind him. Terrance let out a sharp breath, pulling his fisted hands from his pockets, taking in the silence. He lowered his head as he thought of the envelope he wished he could unsee, but he also knew he couldn't ignore any of what was in there.

Too many skeletons hidden by too many people.

Then there was George Schwartz and the conversation he was not looking forward to.

Terrance knew dinner was waiting for him as he stepped off the elevator, seeing the soft lighting, the new table with fresh flowers. He glanced to the left toward Jennifer's suite, taking in the quiet, then turned to the right, toward the suite of George Schwartz. He didn't know why it struck him now when it hadn't before: No expense had been spared in the high-end finishes on this floor alone, from the two custom doors of the penthouse suites to the wallpaper, which was flecked with gold.

Terrance took a step, gripping the envelope he'd kept tucked inside his pickup, remembering well the documents, printed emails, and photos it held. He'd never seen the kind of dirt that was in the envelope he was holding. He made himself take another step toward the door of George Schwartz's penthouse suite, numbered in gold, and he stopped just outside it and hesitated only a second before lifting his hand, fisting it, and knocking.

He put all his attention into listening, and he thought he heard something. His heart was hammering, and he had to shut his wife's face out of his head, because she'd never forgive him if they suddenly didn't have a home.

The door opened, and he looked down at the old man. He'd thought his eyes were blue, but he realized they were brown, yet with nothing warm.

"Terrance, my boy, I didn't expect you."

He'd expected to be invited in, and maybe that was why he felt so awkward. "Sorry, I wanted to give this back to you. You left it for me at the front desk." He held the envelope out.

George didn't pull his gaze as he gestured inside and stepped back. "Come in."

Terrance stepped inside, taking in the hall table and his image in the mirror. He realized for the first time how long his dark hair was. A cut was something he desperately needed.

George closed the door, and Terrance didn't bother with his boots as he waited for the old man to turn around. He didn't know what the hell George was thinking as he stared up at him, wearing a deep red long-sleeve shirt and tan slacks. Then he looked down to the envelope and said, "That's for you to keep. Information is power, especially when you step into any positions of public office."

Terrance willed himself to find the right words. Had anyone ever told this man no? "Sorry, I'm not comfortable with that, and it wouldn't be right." He held out the envelope again and waited, and finally, George reached for it. "And about the council position, I'm afraid I cannot step into something that I wasn't voted into. It just isn't fair…"

The man lifted his hand to stop him. "Terrance, you think you would be voted in? You're a nobody with a ton of baggage, and everything would be used against you to keep you out. You'd be slaughtered before you got out of the gate, with a ton of trouble coming after you, and the people here would see you as a laughingstock forever." He really emphasized the last part, just another kick to his ego.

Terrance only nodded, because he was starting to understand that politics was more about playing a game than actually doing right by the people. Why had he never paid attention before or seen what was so obvious, right in front of him? Maybe because he'd never wanted to know. "I understand that, but still, taking something this way, I can't and won't do it. I'm not using that information. Is that why you gave it to me?"

The old man made a face, and Terrance could see he wasn't happy. Then he let out a rough laugh. "I thought you wanted to help Misty. I guess I read you wrong. The information is for you. Know your enemy, Terrance. You really think anyone gets into office to do the right thing?" George shrugged, and Terrance felt the criticism working its way under his skin.

"The only reason I would take a position on the council is to do the right thing, so I would seriously hope there are more like me out there. No, I don't believe everyone is bad like that. And this isn't about not wanting to help Misty. I will, but not this way. Being part of something underhanded won't fix this. It'll only make another wrong down the road. I can't—no, I won't live with that. I don't plan on being another person in that envelope. I can't be bought, and I will not owe someone. You said I would owe you a favor. I can't, I'm sorry, because the cost would be too high. My integrity."

Damn, he was proud of himself.

George gave him an odd smile. "Your integrity will not keep you and your family warm at night," he said, and a chill ran up Terrance's back.

"Are you telling me that my family and I are going to be on the streets again, out in the cold, because I won't agree to you using me as a puppet?" He couldn't believe how strong he sounded.

George pulled in a breath and then walked around him and settled the envelope on the hall table. Terrance didn't have a clue what he was going to say, and seconds ticked by.

"I offered you an opportunity, is all, to make a difference," George said. "I'm not having you sign your soul over. You're reading way too much into it and are tossing an opportunity away, boy. That's one of the stupidest things, or the bravest, I think I've ever seen someone do.

"You… I'm still figuring you out. You don't want the council position? Fine, I'll put someone else in. But of course I'm not tossing you and your family out onto the streets. One has nothing to do with the other. You don't want my help? You want to play maintenance man here and fix broken plumbing? Be my guest. I thought I saw something in you, Terrance. Guess I was wrong."

The way he said it had sounded so innocent, but Terrance didn't think anything about this man could be trusted.

George looked over and up to him then. "You would let her building be torn down? You would let her sister take everything from her? She's not done, you know. Jennifer won't be happy until she's taken everything from Misty, including every peaceful night's sleep. She takes tremendous pleasure in the destruction of her sister."

Terrance still didn't understand the hate that drove Jennifer. "I'm not letting her do anything. But I can't and won't owe you or use any of that. I'll find another way." He gestured to the envelope, still sick from some of the things he now knew about people that controlled everything in the county. "You said you won't take my job, but you'll stand by and let Jennifer keep kicking at Misty, taking from her. You could stop her."

George gave another odd smile. "We'll be leaving tomorrow. I don't usually spend much time in Montana in the winter." Then he walked to the door, pulled it open, and stood there, and Terrance knew that was his cue to leave. This was likely all he was getting.

He inclined his head and took a step before stopping in the doorway. "Do you mind if I ask you a question?"

He didn't know what to make of the way George was looking at him. He shrugged. "You can."

Terrance looked over to the envelope. "Every one of those people should be in jail, but they're not. Why haven't you given that to the local sheriff?"

George made a face. "You really are naive, Terrance. Is that really what you wanted to ask? You think the local sheriff doesn't already know, or the attorney general? They're small fish looking to move up, and this is too many decades in the making. If a sheriff or boy scout cop who believes in fairy tales looks into someone in office, he'll have his hand slapped by some higher power and shut down. If anyone is suddenly under fire or an investigation happens, it's only because we say so."

He made himself pull in a breath. "You mean if someone suddenly hasn't done as he was told."

The old man smiled without answering.

Terrance knew he was waiting for him to leave. "You're right; that wasn't what I wanted to ask. In this building, I counted all the units, and most are empty, eighty-five percent, yet so many are living on the streets. Why? I don't understand, considering this was supposed to have been built to replace what was torn down for all those folks living out there."

George walked over to the table and reached for the

envelope, then walked it back over to him, holding it out. "Take the envelope. It's yours. Burn it or throw it out. You owe me nothing, Terrance. I didn't expect your integrity. No one has ever done that. Buildings like this are to park money for tax write-offs. You think anyone gives a shit about anyone out there on the street? Those units will never be used. They'll be resold when the market inflates. And all the funding collected from tax-paying citizens to help those people on the streets will continue to go to those who own everything in this world. It's bigger than you, Terrance." He was still holding the envelope out to him.

Terrance finally took it. "What am I supposed to do with this?"

The man blinked, his mouth tight, then gestured as Terrance stepped back out into the hall. "You want to fix anything that's wrong, first you need to know your enemy. Keep your friends close, Terrance, but your enemies closer."

Terrance found himself glancing over his shoulder, seeing nothing. The way George looked past him, he wanted to ask about Jennifer, but he didn't. "Have a good trip," he found himself saying instead as he stepped back, again holding the envelope.

"Word of advice, Terrance: Don't wear your heart on your sleeve. Because when people see how personal something is to you, they'll use it."

Then George closed the door, and Terrance just stared, more confused than ever, because he had no idea whether George was a friend or an enemy.

He could hear his wife in the bedroom with the boys, Greg and John, as he sat in the living room by the gas fireplace. The dishes had long since been put away. Dinner had been fried chicken, which he couldn't remember the last time he'd had.

"You've been pretty quiet since you got home," Lizzie said as she entered the room, wearing a pair of blue jeans and a faded T-shirt, an old sweater pulled overtop.

"You're still too thin," he said.

She made a face as she sat in the easy chair. "And you didn't answer me. Good day, bad day? You were late coming home. You know, Terrance, you don't need to keep things from me."

He was leaning forward now, his forearms resting on his knees. "Just have a lot on my mind, is all. Was offered a position on the city council here today."

Her face lit up.

"Don't get excited," he said. "It came with strings I wouldn't be able to live with. I turned it down. Could have helped Misty keep her building, but I will not owe the kind of people I would owe to do that."

He didn't know what she was thinking. He heard a knock at the door, and he took in the frown on his wife's face. His heart was hammering. Maybe he really had cut his hand off and screwed his family.

"I'll get it." He stood up and made himself start walking. He could hear his wife behind him. He hesitated only a second before pulling open the door and took in the face staring up at him. The dark skin, the scar, the tired eyes, and the gray bomber jacket.

"Misty, what are you doing here?" he said, then glanced over to Kenny, who was standing beside her, his hands in the pockets of his dark jacket.

"Wanted to thank you," she said.

He wondered whether his eyes bugged out. "Come in, please." He stepped back, holding the door as both Kenny and Misty stepped inside. He didn't miss the open question from his wife, who leaned on the island.

"Lizzie, how are you?" Misty said. Kenny only nodded to her.

"I'm good, thank you. I could put on some tea?"

Misty shook her head and lifted her hand as Terrance closed the door. "No, thank you. I just wanted to stop in and thank your husband for what he did."

He still didn't know what she was talking about. "Not sure what I supposedly did," Terrance finally said, pulling his hand over his head and rubbing. "Well, are you going to tell me?"

Misty glanced to Kenny and then back to him. "My building, my shelter, is now open. Was served this today, a notice…" She pulled a piece of paper from her pocket and unfolded it, then held it out to him.

He could see the city letterhead and frowned as he reached for it.

"I had no idea, Terrance, that you were taking over Frank Dumont's position on the city council," she said. "The man has been coming at me and been after me for everything. How did you do it?"

He couldn't look at Misty as he read the letter, which was dated that day, seeing his name as the newly appointed councilor taking over for Frank Dumont. The closure order had been vacated. His heart hammered. He knew this had to be a mistake. He'd just told George no. He made himself shake his head.

"Well, this is good news on the shelter…" he started.

Misty hugged him, and her laughter spilled out. He made himself look over to Kenny, who only nodded, as Misty stepped back and swiped at the dampness under her eyes. She turned and walked the few steps over to his wife.

"This can't be right, though, because I told George no a few hours ago," Terrance said to Kenny. "I won't be bought or owe him a favor. I told him I would only take it honestly after being voted in."

He couldn't make out what his wife was saying, but both women were laughing.

"I don't know what to tell you, Terrance," Kenny said in a low voice. "George is a hard man to read. You may have said no, but he already made the appointment, and as far as he's concerned, you're now the councilor."

He took in the letter again. Kenny reached over and tapped his arm, but he was shaking his head. "No, I'm not. I said no to his terms. I'll have to go up and speak with him again."

Damn, Misty looked so happy, and so did his wife. Kenny glanced back once to them and then stepped closer to Terrance.

"George pulled out not even an hour ago," he said. "You should know that Jennifer is with him, some business in Florida. All I can tell you is that whatever you said didn't make a difference—or maybe it did. He told me before he left with Jennifer that a new maintenance person is going to be hired, and I was supposed to give you this…" He pulled out a set of keys and held them out to him. "It's not the penthouse, but it's on the eighth floor, bigger than this, three bedrooms, fully furnished, for the new councilor and his family."

Terrance took the keys. "He just gave you this, even after I told him no?"

Kenny shrugged and glanced at Misty before turning back to Terrance. "Whatever you said evidently had the old man convinced you're the right person. My advice? Take it, stick to your principles, and move your family up."

"Okay, Kenny," Misty said, striding over. "I want to get on over to my building and get word on the street tonight that I'm back up tomorrow." She rested her hand on Terrance's arm. "I don't know what made you decide to step up, Terrance. All I can say is it seems someone is watching over us. Thank you." Then she reached for the door, pulled it open, and stepped out.

Kenny made to follow her, and with one last look at Terrance, he said, "You'll do fine."

Terrance looked down to the letter and folded it back up, then held it out to him. "So what time do I show up at city hall?"

Kenny reached for the letter with an odd smile. "Nine. Show up at nine."

Then he walked out, and Terrance closed the door. He looked over to his wife, who wore an expression of shock, surprise, something he hadn't seen in a long time, as she walked over to him.

"You forget to tell me something?"

He didn't know if she was furious with him. "I turned it down." He shook his head and stepped over to her, and she ran her hand over his arm. "But I think I could really fix some things."

Lizzie said nothing, just slid her arms over his shoulders, around the back of his neck, and a soft, easy smile touched her lips. "You know what, Terrance? I think you could fix a lot of things."

He leaned down and pressed a kiss to her lips, then pulled her closer. She rested her cheek against his chest as he pulled her into his arms, his chin on top of her head. "So you'd be okay with this?"

He felt her smile against him. Then she pulled back and said, "For the first time in a really long time, Terrance, I feel as if you've put us on the right track. Yeah, I really am okay with this. In fact, I feel so much hope for our future."

He pulled his wife closer again and pressed a kiss to the top of her head. This was something that should have scared him, but he couldn't believe the absolute peace he felt instead.

There was a knock on his open door as he closed up the file containing the city report and budget he'd requested several days ago. Over two months had passed since his first day on the job, and Terrance leaned back in his comfortable office chair and took in the assistant he shared with the other councilors.

"Excuse me, Councilor Mack," she said. "Jennifer Krause is here to see you. I tried to tell her you aren't taking appointments…"

"Oh, he'll see me," Jennifer said from behind her. "Seriously, Terrance, having a minion tell me I have to make an appointment to see the maintenance man I hired?"

Terrance only lifted his hand to Heather, a young woman with light hair and a round face, who had made it clear from day one where her loyalties lay. "It's fine, Heather. I've got it from here. You can close the door behind you," he said, then didn't bother getting up as he took in a woman he knew he'd never like, who strode in wearing high boots and a beige suede jacket that cost more than he'd ever consider spending. There was no smile as she stopped in front of his desk and stared down at him.

"This is quite the move up for you, isn't it?" She rested a black purse on his desk, sat in the chair as if he'd invited her, and pulled off her leather gloves. "You don't take my calls. I'm offended, Terrance. After all, I gave you a place to live, a start. You owe me, buddy." She gestured to him.

"You gave me a job, which I'm grateful for, but I don't owe you anything. You come barging in without an appointment…"

"You listen here, you piece of shit. I don't need an appointment. When I call you, you pick up the phone. You do not want me as your enemy." Her dark eyes flickered, and he knew she could be a serious problem. But he had realized something about her now: She was all about threatening and putting fear into people to get her way.

He narrowed his eyes. "So you're threatening me now? What is it you want, Jennifer?" He glanced over to the closed file, remembering the amount of funding that seemed to be tied up in a shell game. He knew someone had likely gone to a lot of trouble to hide it, or maybe they hadn't expected anyone to really look into it.

"I want that building on the corner," she said. "The proposal I submitted was already approved by the council, but much to my surprise, I see you've flagged it, and now surveyors are saying it has to be preserved for heritage. That is a derelict old eyesore—"

"That belongs to your sister." He cut her off quite calmly, feeling the air sizzle between them. "The building will be preserved. Your proposal will not go anywhere. You want to come after me, go for it. But I won't be bullied or threatened by you." He leaned back in his chair and swiveled to the side, setting his elbow on the armrest. She reached for her purse and rummaged inside before pulling out a thick envelope and tossing it on his desk in front of him. It was letter size, and he would have been a fool not to know what it was.

He didn't reach for it, and he saw she likely hadn't expected his reaction.

"Really, you're not even going to look?" she said. She did have a mean streak.

He reached for the envelope and opened it to see a stack of cash. "So now you're bribing me? No thank you." He tossed the envelope back on the desk in front of her.

"That is a hundred thousand, Terrance. You want more?" She made a rude sound and opened her purse to pull out a checkbook.

"You may as well put that away, too. It could be a million and I still wouldn't take it. You may have bought your way with Frank Dumont, but that won't work with me. Your issues with Misty are not going to be played out on this council anymore."

She didn't reach for the envelope but sat back in the chair and narrowed her gaze as if trying to figure him out. "That money could buy you a home, be a nest egg for you and your family, college for your boys, and you would just toss it away? Stupid, foolish. I think you need to reconsider your options. You think you'll get anywhere on what you make? Seriously, what does a councilor make now—sixty, seventy thousand a year? That's nothing anymore."

He made himself pull in a breath and took in how she leaned forward, how the tension seemed to rise up through her. She was a woman who didn't take no from anyone.

"You like living on the eighth floor in a nice big suite?" she continued. "You think I don't know you worked some deal with George?"

"I didn't work any deal with George. I'll tell you the same thing I told him: I will not be bought, nor will I owe anyone. Yes, sure, he gave me the eighth-floor suite, which I'm sure you're aware you don't own. You cannot ask me and my family to leave."

He pulled open his desk drawer and reached for an envelope that had been waiting for him on his first day in the office. It was from George Schwartz, and it detailed his salary, his benefits, and the apartment that came with the job, as well as the expense allowance and the pension he'd earn. He still didn't understand how George continued to have so much influence.

"From George," he said. "I'm also aware of the diversion of funding to Bridgeman Towers, which was supposed to be rebuilt as low-cost housing for those who needed it. It was funded entirely by taxpayers with state and federal grants. You should know that I've ordered a hearing into the misappropriation of funds, and you should also know that I've already filed a grievance with the city for the empty suites privately sold to foreign investors. The committee will likely drag it out, but I'll keep pushing until every unit is turned back over to the people you forced out.

"As for your sister, your bullying her, paying off city officials to issue her bylaw infractions for anything and everything, and hiring thugs to damage her building and create a nuisance all end now. There will be no more police harassment, no more fines, no more bylaw infractions. Frank Dumont may have been your golden boy, but I'm not." He gestured to the envelope. "Now, if you don't mind, I have work to do."

When she didn't stand, he turned around in his chair and rose, and she finally reached for the envelope and jammed it into her purse.

"Why do you do it?" he said.

She flicked her gaze to him and stood up. By the way

she knit her brow, she didn't understand him. "Do what?" There was nothing friendly in her tone.

"Try to hurt Misty. What did she ever do to you? She's trying to help people, and here you are, doing the opposite, trying to destroy them."

She slid her purse over her arm and pulled on her leather gloves. At first, he didn't think she would answer, but then she lifted her gaze to him. "She's in my way," she said so matter of factly that he realized she was serious. "Oh, don't look at me like that, Terrance. Misty is weak. She settles for ordinary, just like my parents. Pathetic. Do you know what it was like, growing up with them, watching my father take a beating, watch people take from us, and they never fought back? My father should have beat them, should have taken from them. He should have hurt their families, their kids. They're all weak, and I can't stand weakness. It's a poison. So you know what I do, Terrance?"

He wasn't sure he wanted to know, as he suspected the person he saw in front of him didn't have an ounce of empathy. "I'm all ears. What do you do, Jennifer?"

There it was, the smile. "If someone gets in my way, I move them. I take their house, their bank account, their family, their life, until they have nothing left. And I enjoy every moment of it."

He realized this woman hated everyone. She didn't look away, and he felt the ripple of energy between them. "You must be very lonely. I feel sorry for you, Jennifer."

She pulled back as if he had slapped her. "You're pathetic, just like my sister," she said. Then she started to the door but stopped as she rested her hand on the doorknob. She shook her head. "I can be a great friend, Terrance," she said, then looked over to him. "Or your worst enemy."

She pulled open the door and let her gaze linger. "You

know, one day, Terrance, George won't be around, and there's one thing you should know about me: I don't ever forget when someone wrongs me." A smile touched her lips when he didn't answer her. "Have a great day."

She lifted her hand in a wave and walked out of his office just as Heather appeared in the doorway, wide eyed.

"Is everything okay?" she said. "She didn't look happy."

Terrance let out a heavy sigh and gave his head a shake. "If she shows up again, she makes an appointment like everyone else, you understand? She's just an overgrown bully who's used to having her way, only this time, she isn't going to get it."

Heather glanced out the door and then back to him and nodded. "You're really not scared of her?"

He looked down to the file and then back to the young woman, who he knew had never been on his side. "Fear is what she wants. It's always what a bully wants."

She seemed to consider something. Then she smiled. "Wow, a councilor who's a street fighter. Who would have thought? You let me know if you need anything, Councilor."

He let his gaze linger for a second and then nodded. "Thanks, Heather, I will."

Then he sat down and reached for the file. Lifting his gaze to the open door, he realized what she had called him, a street fighter.

And he smiled, because he really was, for the people he represented.

Turn the page for a sneak peek of
THE HUNTED the newest release in *THE O'CONNELLS*
Available in print, eBook & audio

The Hunted

THE O'CONNELLS

When two prisoners escape and one is found dead, Marcus O'Connell finds himself being hunted— and the hunter could be someone he trusts.

One late night, Sheriff Marcus O'Connell receives a call about two escaped prisoners considered a danger to the community. A search is underway, and the warden has reason to believe the escaped convicts are headed toward Livingston. An urgent warning is issued: Shoot to kill.

Hours later, Marcus is called to a crime scene. The body of one of the escaped prisoners has been discovered deep in the woods, and the scene has already been lit up, with three prison guards standing over the body, along with the sheriff and deputy from the county over and a tracker with his dogs. A story has been neatly put together, and the group at the scene tries to send Marcus on his way.

Yet one prisoner is still missing. Marcus is told no investigation is necessary, that he should sign off on the case and walk away. But nothing adds up. The problem is that dead men can't talk, and Marcus can't shake the feeling that the story he's being told is a coverup for something far more sinister.

The Hunted

CHAPTER 1

The sound of crickets punctuated the quiet neighborhood. Darkness had settled in, but Marcus needed a minute, as he leaned against the large porch beam, before he could lock up for the night and feel that all was okay in his part of the world. He lifted his hand in a wave to his brother Owen and his wife, Tessa, as they drove away in her small compact. Again, he took in the neighbors' houses. Next door, the lights were off and all seemed quiet.

Ryan and Jenny were already inside their house across the road, and the outside light was now off. Marcus waited for that feeling he got every night before locking up, an assurance that it would be okay for him to lay his head down and go to sleep. He counted heads, making sure everyone was okay, listening to the sounds inside his house, the fussing of Cameron, who was doing his nightly protest against going to sleep.

The screen door squeaked open behind him, and Marcus turned to see his dad step out, wearing blue jeans and a black t-shirt. He heard his mom and Reine talking inside. His dad nodded to him and headed over.

"Your mom is finishing up in the kitchen with Reine and Eva," Raymond said. "That boy of yours is just like you. You always fought your mom and argued every night about how you weren't tired, but a second later you'd be out cold. You didn't know how to stop."

Marcus turned to look back at the street. He was still trying to understand his dad. He leaned against the post on the porch, breathing in the warm summer night. The smell told him tomorrow would be another hot day.

"You were rather quiet tonight," Raymond said. "Everything okay?"

What was he supposed to say? This feeling had come out of nowhere. He couldn't remember ever having felt so unsettled, and he didn't have a clue what had caused it—family, life, something else?

"Just one of those days, you know," Marcus said, unable to find words to explain it.

His dad only nodded. It wasn't lost on Marcus that his dad had been forced to stick around Livingston because his mom had refused to leave her children and grandkids. His dad had a way of seeing everything. Marcus had figured that much out, but a stranger wouldn't have been able to tell, as Raymond never let his gaze linger too long.

Now he did, narrowing his eyes, peering out into the darkness. The stars were out, and a few streetlights were on. "Always the sheriff, looking out to make sure everyone is tucked in, safe," he said. "Expecting trouble?"

Marcus looked over to his dad. Inside, the house phone was ringing, and a second later, it was answered. "You know something I don't?" he said. The sarcasm dripped.

His dad only shrugged. Marcus heard footsteps and pushed away from the post just as the screen door squeaked again, and Reine stepped out, her dark hair pulled back, wearing a peach sundress, barefoot.

"Marcus, it's for you," she said. "It's Therese." She held out the cordless phone.

Marcus didn't look over to his dad, who he knew was watching him in the way only Raymond O'Connell could. Marcus took the portable phone. "Thanks, Reine," he said, then waited as she walked back in the house. He put the phone to his ear, glancing only once to his dad, knowing his deputy called only if there was something he needed to handle. "What's up, Therese?"

"Sorry to call so late, Sheriff, but I have a message from the warden from Montana State. Two prisoners have escaped, and all he said was that they could be headed this way. I was about to call him back…" There was static on the line. His deputy was cutting in and out, as if she were driving.

"Hey, Therese, you're cutting out. You said two prisoners escaped from Montana State?" He was already walking back into the house and taking the stairs two at a time. Upstairs, Charlotte was reading to his son, whom he thought he heard jumping on his bed. Marcus was in his bedroom now, yanking open the closet door and opening the gun safe to retrieve his .357 SIG.

"Sorry, Sheriff," Therese said. "I'm about twenty minutes away, and the cell service is like shit out here. Picked up the message on the way. All it said was that two prisoners escaped. The warden is…"

"Kellogg," Marcus cut in, fastening the holstered gun to the waistband of his jeans. As he closed up the gun safe, he pictured a man he'd met only a few times.

"I missed that part of the message," Therese said. "I'll give him a call and let you know what he says."

Marcus glanced to the open door. His wife now stood

in the doorway. "No, Therese, I've got it," he said. "I'll have Charlotte check the message, and I'll give the warden a call."

She said nothing, and he noted her hesitation.

"Anything else?" he said, realizing it had come out rather short.

"No, that was all," Therese said. "You sure, Sheriff? I don't mind making the call. It may be nothing."

"Or it may be a lot," he said. "No, I've got this one." Then he hung up and held the phone out to Charlotte, taking in her wide eyes.

"What's going on, Marcus?"

He reached for his badge. "Prison break or something along those lines. Therese just called, said the warden at Montana State left a message. Two prisoners. I need you to get his number and play that message for me."

She was already nodding and dialing the office. Something about his wife handling phones and dispatching again settled him in ways he couldn't explain. She scribbled down the number on a pad of paper on the dresser just as his two-year-old son came running in, all smiles, appearing nowhere near ready to go to sleep.

Marcus reached for him and gave him a toss in the air, then held him and kissed his cheek. "Hey, you. Giving your mom a hard time? You're supposed to be asleep."

"Not tired."

"Yeah, well, you will be soon. Go get a book and get in bed."

"Here, Marcus, the number," Charlotte said. "The message is kind of garbled, but yes, it's something about two prisoners escaping."

He put Cameron down after kissing him again and reached for the paper and the phone, shaking his head over his rambunctious son.

Charlotte shook her head. "He's going to be the end of me. You know he argues every night about how he isn't tired?" She pulled her arms over her faded green t-shirt, her dark hair pulled up in a ponytail. "You're heading out, aren't you?"

"Yeah, after I call the warden," he said. "I don't like this."

There it was, that smile of hers he loved. She leaned in the doorway, glancing once over her shoulder down the hall to where their son's bedroom was as he dialed the phone.

"Montana State, warden's office." The voice was muffled, and Marcus had to really listen past the rough twang.

"This is Sheriff O'Connell, from Livingston. Is the warden there? I've got a message from him about a prison escape."

He heard a rustle on the other end, then a clunk. Evidently, whoever had answered barely knew how to use a phone. "Yeah, yeah," the person said, then yelled out, "Warden! Call for you from that Sheriff O'Connell."

Marcus reached for his wallet and stuffed it in his back pocket, then reached for his duty belt. Charlotte didn't look away, gesturing for an explanation, but Marcus only shook his head. There was another rustle on the phone.

"Sheriff? Warden Kellogg here." The man had a deep voice. "Afraid two prisoners escaped. Was discovered only a short time ago by one of the guards. We're in lockdown now. Just finished a count and are interrogating some prisoners. We know two got out for sure, but how, we have no idea. They likely had help from inside. I suspect they could be headed your way. These men are dangerous, both of them. I've already contacted state officials, as well, along with the other sheriffs in the area. An order has already been issued: Shoot to kill."

Marcus angled his head, looking right at Charlotte. He wasn't sure he'd heard the warden correctly. "You can't be serious," he said. "Who authorized that order? With all due respect, Warden, capturing the prisoners is the first priority."

"Sheriff O'Connell, these prisoners are a danger to the community," the warden said. "They will slit your throat and kill you without a second thought. If you want to dance around them and be the nice guy, do it on your own time and not at the detriment of the good people of Montana. You see them, you shoot them, because these two will do anything and everything to avoid capture. Killing, maiming, looting, burning. You want the details of what they'd do to your wife and sisters, everyone in your family, everyone you care about? If you want to argue with me about bringing them in alive, you can do it, but I don't want these two getting anywhere near innocent people. I've already reached out to Judge Harris, and photos of the prisoners have been sent to you."

Marcus didn't have a clue who these two prisoners were or what they'd done, but that sick feeling was back in his stomach with the image of the horror the warden had painted. Damn, what kind of evil had the two men done?

On the other end, the warden was talking to someone else. Then he addressed Marcus again. "Anything else, Sheriff? If not, I suggest you get your ass out there and start looking. Stan has faxed over the photos, and emails have gone out statewide."

Something about Warden Kellogg had always unsettled Marcus, but he couldn't put his finger on what it was. "Yeah, you said they could be headed my way. Why is that?

They have family, friends, contacts here? I need all that information."

"Everything about both prisoners has been sent to you. One has a girlfriend, I understand, outside Livingston, and a brother up toward Billings. If that's all, Sheriff, I've got a fucking mess to handle here. You have any questions, get in touch with Sheriff Lester up in Stillwater County. He's got more on them, and he's been on this since word went out. And, Sheriff O'Connell? A word of advice. I understand you may want to give these men a second chance, but sometimes we're all better off if a criminal is six feet under. You understand?"

Yeah, he understood, but a knot twisted in his stomach as he looked over to his wife. He wondered if this explained the sick feeling he had or the cold sweat that had broken out up his spine. "Understood," he said. "I'll start looking." Then he hung up and tossed the phone on the bed.

"What is it, Marcus?"

Marcus counted the extra clips in his duty belt, then walked over to his wife and ran his hand over her shoulder. "Warden says the prisoners had help from the inside to get out. Says they're dangerous. Photos have been faxed and emailed. Can you access those? I'm going to ask Mom and Dad to stay until I get back," he said. It was just a feeling he had, the need to keep his family together. "See if you can pull up the prisoners' files, too. Warden said they've been sent. I want to know everything about them: who they are, what they did, and exactly how dangerous they are."

He hurried down the stairs, and Charlotte was right behind him. Raymond was back in the house, and he could hear his mom, Reine, and Eva in the kitchen.

Marcus stepped off the bottom step, and Charlotte moved around him into the living room, over to the small desk where her laptop was.

"What's going on?" Raymond said as Marcus reached for his sheriff's jacket and lifted it from the hook.

"Marcus, I just sent the photos and files to your phone," Charlotte called out.

Marcus pulled his iPhone from his coat pocket and turned to his dad. "Can you and Mom stay?"

Raymond didn't seem surprised. He only nodded and said, "Yeah, of course. You worried about something?"

Marcus pulled out the keys to his cruiser. "Two prisoners have escaped and could be headed this way. Warden says they're dangerous, so much so that he wants us to shoot first and ask questions later, so I don't want to leave Charlotte, Reine, and the kids alone."

He knew his dad understood. "Yeah, you got it," he said. "You be careful."

Marcus thumbed through his phone and pulled up the photos his wife had sent. One was dark skinned, the other lighter, both with dark hair and brown eyes, the same bugged-out mugshot expressions. Their names were Rafe Jackson and Holter Donnelly. "Charlotte, send these to Harold and Ryan, too," he called out over his shoulder as he opened the door, and his dad was right behind him, holding the inside screen. "Charlotte has the photos," Marcus told him. "Take a good look."

Raymond nodded. "I'll call Ryan and Owen," he said.

Marcus lingered just outside. He didn't know what to say to his dad. Out of anyone, he knew Raymond had a handle on this. "Thanks," he finally said, then started down the steps. He heard the door close behind him and the lock flick closed.

He dialed his cell phone, walking straight for his cruiser and climbing in. As he tossed his duty belt and coat on the passenger seat, the phone rang once, twice…

"Okay, what did you forget?" Suzanne answered. He thought he heard Arnie fussing in the background.

"Put Harold on," he said, shoving his cell phone in the mount on the dash. He started the car.

"No can do," Suzanne said. "He's in the shower. What is it?"

There she went, playing interference. He knew she was still pissed at him because he wouldn't let her play cop in his county.

"You tell Harold to get the hell out of the shower and call me back," he said. "There was a prison break. This is serious shit, Suzanne. Charlotte just sent him the photos and files. I need him to dig into it and then meet me at the office. I'm not messing around. Have him call me. Can you do that?"

She was quiet for a second. "Don't take my head off, Marcus. Yeah, I'll tell him. Hey, big brother?" She always seemed to need to have the last word.

"What?" he said as he backed the cruiser out, ready to get off the phone. He flicked on the headlights and gave the vehicle gas, looking out into the darkness, knowing he'd be taking a second and third look at anyone he saw that night, scrutinizing who they were and what they were doing.

"Watch your back," she said.

He felt a smile tug at the corners of his lips. "Always do," he said. "Now have Harold call me."

Marcus ended the call before his sister could add one more thing. As he rounded the corner, feeling his own angst, he drove slower than usual and took a good, long look at the few pickups parked along the street, scanning for anyone out walking. There was only a couple with a dog.

This was going to be a really long night.

"Lorhainne Eckhart is one of my go to authors when I want a guaranteed good book. So many twists and turns, but also so much love and such a strong sense of family."

(LORA W., REVIEWER)

New York Times & USA Today bestseller Lorhainne Eckhart is best known for writing Raw Relatable Real Romance where "Morals and family are running themes." As one fan calls her, she is the "Queen of the family saga." (aherman) writing "the ups and downs of what goes on within a family but also with some suspense, angst and of course a bit of romance thrown in for good measure."

Follow Lorhainne on Bookbub to receive alerts on New Releases and Sales and join her mailing list at Lorhainne-Eckhart.com for her Monday Blog, all book news, give-aways and FREE reads. With over 120 books, audiobooks, and multiple series published and available at all, retailers now translated into six languages. She is a multiple recipient of the Readers' Favorite Award for Suspense and Romance, and lives in the Pacific Northwest on an island, is the mother of three, her oldest has autism and she is an advocate for never giving up on your dreams.

"Lorhainne Eckhart has this uncanny way of just hitting the spot every time with her books."

(CAROLINE L., REVIEWER)

The O'Connells: *The O'Connells of Livingston, Montana are not your typical family. A riveting collection of stories surrounding the ups and downs of what goes on within a family but also with some suspense, angst and of course a bit of romance thrown in for good measure. "I thought I loved the Friessens, but I absolutely adore the O'Connell's. Each and every book has different genres of stories, but the one thing in common is how she is able to wrap it around the family, which is the heart of each story." (C. Logue)*

The Friessens: *An emotional big family romance series, the Friessen family siblings find their relationships tested, lay their hearts on the line, and discover lasting love! "Lorhainne Eckhart is one of my go to authors when I want* *a guaranteed good book. So many twists and turns, but also so much love and such a strong sense of family." (Lora W., Reviewer)*

The Parker Sisters: *The Parker Sisters are a close-knit family, and like any other family they have their ups and downs. Eckhart has crafted another intense family drama… "The character development is outstanding, and the emotional investment is high…" (Aherman, Reviewer)*

The McCabe Brothers: *Join the five McCabe siblings on their journeys to the dark and dangerous side of love! An intense, exhilarating collection of romantic thrillers you won't want to miss. — "Eckhart has a new series that is definitely worth the read. The queen of the family saga started this series with a spin-off of her wildly successful Friessen series." From a Readers' Favorite award—winning author and "queen of the family saga" (Aherman)*

Lorhainne loves to hear from her readers! You can connect with me at:
www.LorhainneEckhart.com
lorhainneeckhart.le@gmail.com

In the Family
In the Silence
In the Charm
Unexpected Consequences
It Was Always You
The First Time I Saw You
Welcome to My Arms
Welcome to Boston
I'll Always Love You
Ground Rules
A Reason to Breathe
You Are My Everything
Anything For You
The Homecoming
Stay Away From My Daughter
The Bad Boy
A Place of Our Own
The Visitor
All About Devon
Long Past Dawn
How to Heal a Heart
Keep Me In Your Heart

The O'Connells
The Neighbor
The Third Call
The Secret Husband
The Quiet Day
The Commitment
The Missing Father
The Hometown Hero
Justice
The Family Secret

The Fallen O'Connell
The Return of the O'Connells
And The She Was Gone
The Stalker
The O'Connell Family Christmas
The Girl Next Door
Broken Promises
The Gatekeeper
The Hunted

The McCabe Brothers
Don't Stop Me (Vic)
Don't Catch Me (Chase)
Don't Run From Me (Aaron)
Don't Hide From Me (Luc)
Don't Leave Me (Claudia)
Out of Time

A Billy Jo McCabe Mystery
Nothing As it Seems
Hiding in Plain Sight
The Cold Case
The Trap
Above the Law
The Stranger at the Door
The Children
The Last Stand
The Charity

The Wilde Brothers
The One (Joe and Margaret)
The Honeymoon, A Wilde Brothers Short
Friendly Fire (Logan and Julia)

Not Quite Married, A Wilde Brothers Short
A Matter of Trust (Ben and Carrie)
The Reckoning, A Wilde Brothers Christmas
Traded (Jake)
Unforgiven (Samuel)
The Holiday Bride

Married in Montana

His Promise
Love's Promise
A Promise of Forever

The Parker Sisters

Thrill of the Chase
The Dating Game
Play Hard to Get
What We Can't Have
Go Your Own Way
A June Wedding

Kate & Walker

One Night
Edge of Night
Last Night

Walk the Right Road Series

The Choice
Lost and Found
Merkaba
Bounty
Blown Away: The Final Chapter
He Came Back

The Saved Series

Saved
Vanished
Captured

Single Titles
Loving Christine